FIRST SEASON

Harrisburg Railers, book 2

_____

RJ SCOTT
V.L. LOCEY

Love Lane Books

Copyright

Dedication

To Rj – aka the other half of the Wonder Twins - for filling my days with laughter, friendship, and a newfound love of the craft that I had thought I'd lost. To Jean, Ellie, Cathy, and Kathleen, for talking me down and lifting me up. And, of course, to my husband and daughter who stood by my side through the year that shall not be named. My thanks to all of you for guiding me back to the joy of words. ~ V.L. Locey

To Vicki for another three weeks of fun, and to making me laugh so hard over the most *twins* of things. To all my fellow hockey fans who are as gutted as me that we have to wait until October for the season to restart! And always for my family. ~ RJ Scott

With grateful thanks to Meredith for her beautiful cover, Rebecca for making us look good, Rachel for sorting us out, and our army of proofers for their hard work.

FIRST season

— HARRISBURG RAILERS 2 —

RJ SCOTT &
V.L. LOCEY

Love Lane Books

ONE

Layton

This was turning out to be the worst day of my life. Worse even than the time the football team decided to shove me in a locker, and then wedge the door shut.

Everything started out okay. The Railers appointment was my third job since leaving college and choosing to specialize in crisis management. Call me a spin doctor or a marketing guy, it doesn't matter; I was there with my bright, shiny degree in business in my back pocket, to solve a problem using social media, training, and careful planning.

"We want to hire you, but are you gay?" The caller asked when he contacted me.

He couldn't really ask me that, but at that point, with bills to pay, I worded it a lot better than just blurting out a "*What the hell?*"

"I'm not sure how that's relevant," I said.

The man on the other end of the phone, who hadn't even identified himself, just that he worked for a hockey team, sighed noisily. "Fucked if I know," he said. "I just need someone to help us through this."

So I asked him what he meant, and at the point when he completely lost his shit over whether to use the word homosexual in a press release, I decided to give him the benefit of the doubt.

"I can handle this," I reassured him. "You need me."

I didn't care how I got it, I just knew that I was the best person for the job.

He told me he was the GM for the Railers hockey team, and even though my heart sank and my chest tightened, I had to do this. A hockey team, a player coming out of the closet—this was a high-value client.

I did my research after the call; I didn't watch hockey, but I knew of it, and it was basically a bunch of jocks on skates. Right? They needed to be told when to talk and when not to talk, and what was appropriate and when. I could do that. Add in the fact that I would be managing the first official coming-out in the hockey world, and this could make or break my career. I could become a crisis management expert in the field of sports.

The irony of that didn't escape me, given my past.

I had breakfast, wore my newest suit, a crisp white shirt and a brand new blue tie to match the team colors. I'd shaved off my non-ironic loggers' beard, and my man bun was gone. I felt a little naked, but I wanted to be taken seriously, and what used to be hot in styling now seemed to be the butt of jokes. I didn't want to be the butt of anyone's jokes.

Honestly, I'd thought of everything.

Except.

Walking into the East River Arena, home of the Harrisburg Railers hockey team, freaked me out. It was the smell, I think, and the cavernous expanse of seats. I could imagine the shouting, the jeering, the excitement, and all of that became a ball of fear inside me.

Jocks. I can handle them. They're adults now, and I'm not the same nerdy kid I used to be.

Still, it didn't stop me losing my breakfast in the first bathroom I could find off the tunnel from the parking garage. So much for eating to give me energy. I was a wrung-out mess, clinging to porcelain and wishing I could get a handle on my nerves. I'd had two clients before this, big companies with interesting problems, where my lectures on sensitivity awareness had been well received. I could handle rough feedback, crappy tweets, Facebook discussions about inappropriate shit, but they were corporate clients, not hockey players.

It was me and them.

Alone.

Talking one-on-one with hockey players and the support network around them about how it was okay for one of their players to be sleeping with their coach. Also that gay was good, love was love, and oh yeah, could they stop tweeting shit about anything to do with gender, politics, and sexual orientation, to name three things on my list.

These guys were jocks. Well-paid jocks, with a whole army of fans who hung on their every word. The captain had over eighty thousand Twitter followers, mostly because he seemed to be the poster boy for sex on skates. Lots of tweets with videos of him half naked. Not to mention Ten's Instagram, which was new, but which already had an explosion of followers, probably for the same reason—he was hot, and a skater. I noticed links to a lot of websites that featured the hottest men in hockey. Without knowing it, Ten and the team captain were probably gay icons. Go figure.

And it was for Ten and his boyfriend that I was here. Ten was the hotshot on the Railers team, one of those players who were making a mark on the NHL. Or so the press releases said. All I saw was a gay man coming out in a hostile sports environment and that was what I was dealing with.

Ten, hockey player, and his partner, Jared, coach, were in a committed relationship and I had to make people see that this was normal. Okay. A good thing.

I can do this. I am strong. I will not be sick again.

I relaxed each tight muscle and swallowed around the dryness in my throat. Today was going to go well. Why would anything go wrong? I'd prepared what I needed, researched enough about the team to know the personnel, if not the game of hockey itself; there was only so much I could do in the week since I'd been called to do this job. I even had an office, apparently.

So I'd been sick; lots of people got sick before significant events. I could handle being sick.

Which was exactly when things went even more wrong. I turned the tap on to wash my hands, and the damn thing was fierce and splashed my pants. I jumped back in shock and horror, and smacked myself on the door to a stall, the brunt of my weight taken by my left hip.

"Fuck," I cursed, and turned off the water. There was no hand dryer, just paper towels, and I dabbed my pants, painfully conscious that my first meeting with team management was in ten minutes.

I rubbed at the wetness, then realized some of the water had splashed my briefcase as well. That was the moment I wondered if the morning could get any worse.

Which was when the door opened and I swung, startled, to face the newcomer, my briefcase swinging as well and catching the man in the thigh.

"Jesus," I snapped, angry with myself, then let out a small, "I'm sorry."

Tall and Growly stared at me in shock, muscles tensed, and rubbed his thigh. "What the fuck?" was all he said.

He was wearing a Railers T-shirt, but I didn't recall him from my research, so if he was a player then he couldn't be one of the big names I needed to know about to start with. Maybe he was a trainer?

"Sorry," I repeated.

He stared at me, then looked me up and down with a very careful, disdainful look. Or at least I thought it was disdainful; he looked for a moment like he was checking me out, but that wasn't possible given that we were in a hockey arena. He was gorgeous—blue eyes, his red hair styled but soft, his jawline square, and his body broad.

Then the disdain, or whatever it was, turned into a sly wink, and he gestured at my crotch.

"Hey buddy, you might want to make time for a potty break sooner if you have such a teeny bladder. Just saying."

I blinked at him, not knowing what to say. I mean, did I stand there and explain about the tap, or the water, or falling back against the stall door, or even that I'd just lost my breakfast?

I couldn't say any of it. I picked up my jacket from the small table by the door and shoved past him and out into the hall. A few seconds later I was at the door marked "Staff," and pressed the button to get in.

"Railers Hockey," a voice came through the speaker by the door.

"Layton Foxx," I said, and caught sight of the bathroom guy walking my way. The door buzzed, I pushed it open, shut it quickly behind me, and hoped to hell that would give me breathing space.

A short woman stood waiting with a welcoming smile on her face and holding out a hand. I shook it, realizing at the last moment that mine was damp.

"Jane Monroe, PA to Felix Cote, team owner."

She didn't react to the damp on my hand, but when I pulled it away I was flustered.

"Sorry, I had a thing," I began, then cleared my throat, which was raw from vomiting, "with the bathroom faucet," and I waved at my crotch.

Her lips twitched into a smile. "This way, Mr. Foxx, management is expecting you."

Fuck my life.

THE DAY DIDN'T GET MUCH BETTER. The management team had been a nervous, twitchy, bunch, and worried about the big picture. I hadn't entirely got the sense that they had an issue with the gay hockey player thing, but their bottom line was revenue.

The brief had expanded from supporting Ten and Jared to ensuring that revenue wasn't harmed.

Great, nothing like moving the goalposts on my first day and setting unrealistic expectations.

At least Felix Cote had been supportive; I often found changes in any group had to be supported by the person at the top. He'd made some veiled comments about how things had been "in his day," but I could work with that.

Tennant Rowe and Jared Madsen were going to make my career or destroy it in one go, that much was obvious. Now, looking at them sitting opposite me, at the way they unconsciously leaned toward each other, worried me. As a gay man who'd been out to his family and friends since he was sixteen, I couldn't imagine what it must be like to have to hide who you are, but that was the playing field in professional sports, no pun intended.

These two—one a coach on the team, the other a professional hockey player in his prime—had fallen in love.

Not only that, but they'd decided it was time to come out, and the Railers had hired me to manage the fallout.

Because there would be fallout, that much was certain.

"It's going to come at you from all directions," I said.

Tennant frowned at me. His emotions were written plainly on his face. He was angry, defensive, scared, happy, positive and negative, all in one horrible mess. The only thing I could pin down was that he was absolutely in love with Jared and completely convinced of what he wanted to do.

"Go on," Jared said, and he laced his fingers with Ten's. They could in here—we were alone, the three of us, with the door closed and no cameras. But this was the first thing they needed to handle.

"You need to be careful with public displays of affection."

I saw two very different reactions. Jared looked resigned and nodded, but Ten bristled with the start of genuine indignation. I knew what he was going to say, and I headed him off at the pass.

"It shouldn't matter," I began, choosing my words carefully, "But this isn't going to be easy. There will be the religious fans deciding you're going against God, right down to the parents who don't want their kids exposed to non-heteronormative behavior. The spectrum of reaction will be varied. You'll get some who advocate for you, the team, the management, and fans who don't give a shit what you do in your private time as long as Ten is scoring goals."

"We know that," Jared said.

"We don't have to like it," Ten said, and his tone was worrying. He sounded miserable, and he was fully leaning against Jared.

I shuffled the papers on the desk, lining them up to give myself time to think. I'd managed personal clients before, polished them as a product, managed their every moment until they learned how to act in public and how to make the best of who they were. Only, those had been people who needed to clean up their act. I'd helped the telecom company with their painful downsizing, and a college with an equality issue. I was the best at what I did, and I worked hard to make things right for people. But this? The two of them didn't have to come out publicly; they could go on being the secret that wasn't a secret, at least until Ten's playing days were done. He might be only twenty-two, but a professional career doing what these players did was often over by their early thirties. Sometimes sooner, I thought when I recalled that a heart problem had sidelined Jared from his professional career. Ten would only have to wait another decade or so to retire. Was that something he'd be willing to do? I had to ask the question, and hoped I didn't lose the confidence of either man.

"You could stop this now," I said bluntly.

Jared was the first to speak. "I know, but we won't stop."

Ten bit his lip. "We want this."

I nodded and looked down at my notes, but I didn't need them. I'd had my own share of prejudice in life; plenty of life experience to tap from.

"The press will love you and hate you equally. If the Railers lose, it will be reported widely in different ways. The quality press may well suggest that Ten was distracted, with the implication being that Jared here is the distraction. The gossip sites could suggest that maybe you're having too much gay sex with your gay coach. On the other hand, if you win, it could be suggested that you freaked out the other team, that maybe they didn't want to be near you. Then there are the really shitty things they can say. They could bring up skating accidents, blood, HIV

—it might not stop with criticism about your sexual orientation, but could become something bigger."

"And on a positive note?" Jared asked dryly.

"Sorry." I sat back in my chair. "I needed to explain that to you up front."

"We already know all that," Ten said tiredly.

"And I'm here as your supporter in this. We're in open dialogue with various equality-in-sports groups—"

"Locker rooms should be safe and sports venues should be free from homophobia. Athletes should be judged on talent, heart and work ethic, not sexual orientation and/or gender identity." Ten mumbled the whole mission statement of one of the biggest groups advocating for equality.

"That's what we're aiming for."

"Okay, so where do we start?" Ten said, and gripped Jared's hand tight.

"I'm not big into hockey," I began.

Jared looked shocked. Ten's mouth fell open.

"But that doesn't stop me understanding the social and economic issues we're facing with this."

"You don't like hockey?" Ten said incredulously, like that wasn't a possible thing in his world.

"It isn't important to know the game to be aware of the culture."

"That's crap." That was from Jared, who shook his head. "I'll sit you down and explain a few things, and you need to sit in on games. If you don't get hockey, then…" He paused and searched for the right words. "You don't *get* hockey."

"It's on my list," I reassured him.

"Seriously? No hockey at all?" Ten asked again.

I decided to change the subject. "First off, I need to find out a bit more about both of you. Ten, I understand you have two brothers who also play hockey?"

The meeting was long, but by the time we'd got to the end of it I had a picture of the sort of thing I was up against. We had a lot of positives going for us. Management was looking to spin the whole coming-out story to their benefit. Being the first NHL team with an out player would either be an incredible marketing option, or cut ticket revenue. They were demanding the first and ignoring the chance of the second. The team was next on my list; I'd be interviewing them singly for short sessions behind closed doors, to ascertain any issues I'd have to deal with. Those started soon, and first up was the captain, Connor Hurley.

"Connor," I said as he stepped in. I shook his hand. "I'm Layton Foxx."

"Nice to meet you, Layton."

Connor was a quiet guy, all serious eyes and focus, and he listened to everything I had to say and asked reasonable, well-thought-out questions. He was one hundred percent behind Ten and Jared, and he was a good guy to have on our side.

"It helps that Ten's brothers have a significant presence on other teams," he said, and I made a note of that. I'd been thinking the same thing. Ten was close with his brothers, and they had his back.

"Do you have any concerns with the team?"

He and I had signed a confidentiality form at the start of the session, as I'd do with the entire team as I saw them one by one. He knew he could speak freely, but in any case he was intense when it came to the team, and he didn't hesitate to sketch me the bigger picture of who each player was and what I should look out for, good and bad. From defenseman, Arvy who had a gay cousin, to a new guy on the team, Adler, who seemed ambivalent about the entire situation. I made so many notes, I knew I'd have to go through them and summarize in places.

I liked the Railers captain, and when we shook hands I thanked him for his time. He took his role as seriously as I took mine, and there was mutual respect there.

After meeting with a few of the other players, I was done for day one. I shuffled all my notes again, lining them up and putting them into my briefcase along with the iPad that was my connection to the outside world. Then I reported in to Emma, the marketing manager for the team and the person alongside whom I'd be working.

She was demonstrably grateful that all that mess hadn't been handed to her, so that meant I'd earned one hell of a lot of brownie points.

There was a small group of guys in the parking area. One I recognized—Stan the Russian, as Captain Hurley called him—was a huge bear of a man, and he was staring as I walked toward them. The direction wasn't deliberate; they were huddled by my car.

"Guys," I said calmly, even though the sight of these big men waiting by my car was enough to have me feeling anxious as memories of old times poked at me. Not to mention that Stan had his thick arms crossed over his chest and looked like he wanted to go to war with me. I recognized two of the others with him—Coach Benning looking grim, Arvy grinning at me —and the other man was the guy from the bathroom.

That was Adler, the one the captain, in my interview with him that morning, had chosen to highlight as "not exactly vocally critical nor entirely supportive."

I was scarlet and I knew it, and Adler smirked at me. Asshole.

He wasn't the first person to smirk at me, and he wouldn't be the last. Adler Lockhart was a good-looking man, but then a lot of the players on this damn team were hot and right on to burning. Take Arvy with his goofy smile and his long wavy hair, or Coach Madsen with his intense blue stare and air of authority.

"Little bit talk," Stan said, his voice loud and booming in the cavernous underground parking.

I glanced from Stan to the others. I wasn't sure Adler wanted to talk. He was still smirking, but at the same time he looked like he was trying to edge away. The only thing stopping him was that he was pinned between Stan, Arvy, and my car.

I glanced at my watch, like I had to assess if I had the time to stop and talk. Of course I had time. Lots of time. All that was waiting for me at my place was takeout and a night of reading my notes. Oh, and catching up on the hundred or so Facebook messages from my family.

"I can give you five minutes," I said, to qualify the importance of my time and reinforce my status. It was vital that I didn't join in with discussions outside the official meetings; I had to stay outside the hockey circle, so that I could maintain a perspective on how things were playing out. Informal meetings didn't get things done.

Stan pulled aside his shirt and showed me a tattoo. I had to peer closely, because I wasn't sure what I was looking at, or even why it was being shown to me. It looked like a cartoon character; a Pokémon or something.

"Hulk," Stan said, and looked at me expectantly like I was supposed to understand a word. I don't speak any Russian, though, so I looked at Coach for help.

"What he's saying," Coach Benning said, "is that he likes Ten, a lot, and that Ten and he had tattoos the same day, and that if you end up hanging Ten out to dry, then he will have something to say about it and go all Hulk on your ass." The coach's tone was easy, but there was a thread of steel in there.

"You got all that from one word?" I asked, and looked up at Stan, who was still scowling.

Coach only smiled. "He's a man of few words. English ones, anyway."

Stan clapped a hand on my shoulder, and jeez, he was one strong man. For a split second, fear skittered through me, but I pushed the fear back down where it belonged. No one here was going to hurt me.

I edged out of Stan's reach and offered up my most reassuring smile. Stan looked at me, and then he smiled as well.

Seemed like we had an agreement going.

"Are we done talking about cock now?" Adler said loudly, breaking the accepting vibe in the small group. He underscored the words by grabbing suggestively at his groin. "Unless we're whipping them out."

"Jesus Christ, Ads," Arvy snapped, and elbowed him.

Adler grinned. "All I'm saying is some of us have actual sex to go home to and don't spend all day jawing about it."

Then he shoved his way past Arvy, who shoved him back before letting him go.

"Asshole," Arvy muttered, but it wasn't said with heat. I exchanged glances with him, and he gave that single-shoulder shrug of "What can you do?"

I mentally added Adler to my list of concerns.

THE DRIVE HOME was one of my better commutes, the traffic not too heavy and an audio book a quiet background for my thoughts. I liked music, but sometimes just the drone of words was enough to allow me to center and collect everything together.

I'd been lulled into a false sense of security today, or at least that was what I decided. Everyone had been so accommodating, thoughtful, and encouraged by my words… and then there was Adler. I knew the team was facing a rocky few months, maybe longer, but random comments about cock were not what I was looking for.

I looked up his bio as soon as I walked through the door; he was the one I needed to watch. Apart from his name, there were all kinds of complicated stats, which I made a good guess at and looked the rest up online.

ADLER KINCAID LOCKHART

Born Nov. 4, 1993, Brampton, Maine
6'4 219 lbs.
Left Wing—shoots Left
Last Season—GP 57 – G 31– A 23 – P 54– Plus/Minus 5 – PIM 51 – PPG 19 – GWG 4 – OTG 3- S% 18.2

SEEMED PRETTY STRAIGHTFORWARD.

I'd met guys like him before. Either he'd been checking me out that morning and he was in the closet, or he was a homophobic asshole and didn't give a shit who knew it. He'd used the word cock today, and been highly suggestive, so I made some notes about appropriate language, against his name in particular and the rest of the team in general.

CHINESE ORDERED, I sat at the table and decided I'd put off checking family messages long enough. No doubt it would be the typical inane run of news about Zach and Adam and their plumbing business, or David complaining about the economy affecting construction and his electrician business, or maybe it would be Louise talking about daycare and how she wished sometimes that working in daycare didn't involve children.

Then again, it could be my mom, worrying about me being the only one not living in the old hometown. My moving away from Alton Heights, Michigan, and attending NYU had been both something to be proud of and something to worry her. Add on the fact that I'd never gone home after college, instead buying a place in Harrisburg, and I was apparently the reason she had gray hair.

Privately, I wasn't the only one of her five children who knew she dyed her hair every four weeks, regular as clockwork, to keep it flawlessly blonde. She was a homemaker—you name it and she did it in the name of looking out for the family. Bake sales, community events, dinner on the table every night at six, she did it all.

I answered Zach's message about Mom's seventieth birthday event. "Yes, I'll be there, tell me when." I replied to David and Louise in a similar way, because it seemed three out of four of my siblings were convinced I wouldn't turn up to Janet Foxx's party.

I loved my mom. After my dad died ten or so years ago she'd been there for me as much as she could, and there was no way I'd miss the event.

Adam's message was just one long joke about a rabbi in a bar and didn't really make sense. I typed LOL anyway, and hoped that it was funny and not some serious story about an actual rabbi he'd met in a bar.

So when the Chinese arrived and I'd tipped it onto a plate, I had one more person to talk to, and I thumbed through my contacts for Mom, steeling myself to answer all the usual questions.

"Finally my baby calls," she said by way of a hello. "I

nearly sent Zach to find out if you were still alive. You never call, you never visit…"

Wow, she hadn't waited long to lay the guilt over me. "Mom, you know I'd come back if I could."

"You still working with that actor?"

"No, with a hockey team now, as a social media awareness and crisis management support officer."

"A what now?"

"A social—"

"Oh," she interrupted. "You should talk to David about hockey. You remember Calvin, his friend from junior high? Well his cousin's friend's brother… or was it his brother's cousin? Wait, that wouldn't make sense, would it? Anyhow, this young boy has moved lock stock and barrel up north, playing for some team."

North to my mom meant Canada, and no, I didn't recall a Calvin, or know what the hell she was talking about. I'm the youngest of five children, with a big gap between me and the next sibling up, Louise, my only sister. Mom and Dad had me late—she was forty-four and pregnant with her fifth, and now, as I neared twenty-six, my strong-as-an-ox mom was reaching her seventieth. All those years she'd given me and my siblings meant I could stand to listen to her rambling on about a kid I didn't know.

"So you got a boyfriend yet?"

That blindsided me, the question coming out of nowhere, and entirely separate from the subject of Calvin's kind-of-cousin who played hockey.

"No, Mom," I said.

"You just dating casually?" she asked.

I cut her off before she began to ask me about my sex life, and believe me, she loved asking about that. "Yes, a hockey player," I lied.

"Good. I want to see you enjoying life."

"I do, Mom."

"So are you coming for my surprise party next month?"

"Mom, jeez," I spluttered. "You're not supposed to know about that."

"Oh, so there is one, then."

Shit. I'd just been played by my mother.

"No," I said, but it really was too late. "Mom, I have to go; my takeout has arrived."

"Okay, Layton. You take care, now, and call me more often."

"I will, Mom."

Guilt at lying to her poked at me insistently, but I tried to ignore it. I shoveled in a fork of noodles and opened my iPad with my other hand, typing a quick message to Louise, who I knew was the chief organizer of Mom's birthday, admitting what had happened. There wasn't an immediate reply; I hadn't expected one.

Between my four siblings, there were four spouses and at last count, ten children, Louise leading the pack with five children all by the age of thirty-one, the youngest only a couple of months old now.

I was seriously the odd one out in that family.

The only one to go to college and get a degree, the only one with a career that pulled in good money, the only one who moved away.

I went to bed with a hundred questions in my head, all focused around the Railers and my plans for the team. First off I needed to talk to each player, and I moved Adler Lockhart up the list.

I got the feeling that the gorgeous man with the come-to-bed eyes and the seriously un-PC attitude was the one to watch.

TWO

Adler

I crawled behind the wheel of my car, the seat of the BMW 540i cradling my stupid, sorry ass like a finely crafted Italian leather driving glove, of which I had a pair floating around in there somewhere. Maybe in the trunk? Who knew. And more importantly, who cared? I looked at myself in the rearview.

"You are literally the biggest bag of dicks ever to suck air, Adler," I told my reflection. The dude in the mirror totally agreed.

I slammed the driver's side door shut. My forehead met the steering wheel. What the hell was my issue? Why did I always do this? Meet a hot guy, make some crack about his bladder control, feel like an ass, then compound my asshole status by making an even *worse* joke when I saw the incredibly hot man a second time.

"Massive bag of dicks," I murmured as I bounced my brow off the wheel a few times.

When the pain started to set in, I stopped with the head-banging. It didn't feel right without music anyway. I cranked up the Poison CD in the top-of-the-line stereo system, then proceeded to blow my eardrums up. Nothing like Bret Michaels and C.C. Deville to jam your blues away. Pity even C.C. wasn't working this time. That was when you knew it was bad. 80s hair bands cured every ill ever.

I cranked over the engine and threw the Beemer into gear. Time to go home. Eat. Grab a nap. Drown myself in the shower.

"Note to self. Check best way to drown in shower without actually dying, because Santa is coming soon and yay, Christmas." Pfft.

Driving to my condo, I ran over the day and groaned yet again. I was trying too hard. I knew it. That was Adler, though. *Sing, dance, and toss out stupid jokes like a jester because of that one time Dad thought your knock-knock joke was clever.*

KNOCK KNOCK!

Adler, please, I'm trying to work. Go find Apollo and pester him.
Knock knock!
Fine, okay, who's there?
Oswald.
Oswald who?
Oswald my bubble gum!
Oswald what?
Not Oswald. I swallowed—it sounds like Oswald.
That's clever, son, now go find Apollo.

I JUMPED when the guy behind me laid on his horn. Shit, how had I gotten down by the capitol building already? Lost in the past would get me wrapped around a telephone pole in the present.

Bret and C.C. were now talking about what the cat had

dragged in. Great song. Fuck my life. Shit. I'd need to find a way to make that poor stiff stud smile tomorrow. Maybe I could lay that great Oswald knock-knock joke on him, because it had worked so many wonders with Dad. Not.

Home came into view. I swung into the parking lot and sat in my designated spot after cutting the engine.

The Executives. Twenty elite condominiums for those with executive tastes. And executive-sized trust funds, one of which I possessed. Money was not an issue for the Lockhart family. Dad was a legend in the field of corporate takeovers. Mom was a legend in the field of traveling and having affairs to counteract how lonely she was because Dad was always taking over corporations. But hey, I had lots of zeroes in my bank account, and that was what mattered. Money. Spending it and making more of it.

The ride up to my penthouse was agony. Why? Why did they pipe in such shitty elevator music? Why not something from RATT, or maybe a little Winger? Why had that guy at the stadium looked so fucking edgy, and not the avant-garde kind of edgy? Why was his mouth so lush? Why had I asked about his bladder? Fucksticks. I was a butt plug of epic size and girth.

As soon as the doors opened, I stalked across the small lobby that visitors to my prestigious home saw first. It was all decorated and shit. Some guy with pink hair and a tight ass had done it for me when I'd been traded to the Railers. He and I had hooked up once after the condo and lobby had been revamped to his specs. He'd been really picky and totally not my type, but I'd been feeling alone and vulnerable. Also, he'd laughed at my jokes, so that had earned him a good fuck.

I threw my duffel down the moment I stepped into my apartment.

"Lucy, I'm home!" I shouted, then grabbed the bills from the side table. Utilities, mostly. Apollo would handle those. I'd been hoping for maybe a postcard from my parents. Where were they at the moment? France? No. Greece? No. Shit, I couldn't keep track. "Apollo, dude, where are Cole and Karrie Anne?" I never called them mom and dad, they'd demanded I call them Cole and Karrie Anne and I was cool with that. You get used to things after a while.

"They're down in Florida playing golf with the orange troll man until Friday, then they're off to Capri for the holidays."

"Oh yeah." Great. More hand-crafted leather sandals I would never wear.

I padded through my living room. It was all glass and chrome, white and blue. I inhaled deeply and picked up the scent of something celeryish and that coconut-and-melon shampoo Apollo used. Over in the corner were boxes that could only be Christmas decorations. Why did Apollo insist on putting shit up when no one aside from me and him would see the tinsel and tiny little wooden reindeer statues was beyond me. I looked out at the city and sighed at the snow lightly falling. I hadn't had a family holiday since… forever ago.

Stepping into the kitchen, I found Apollo at the stove. He looked over his shoulder and immediately frowned.

"You look like shit. What happened?"

"The bills are here." I whipped them onto the marble counter, then draped a leg over one of three stools at the island.

"Yeah, I know, I brought them up."

Apollo tossed some fresh parsley into his creation with flair. He did everything with flair and a bit of flamboyance.

Apollo Vasquez was my oldest and dearest friend. His mother was head of domestic affairs for my mother's home in Maine, where I'd grown up. Mom owned the four homes in the States, Dad owned the six overseas.

Apollo was my age, twenty-four, and had grown up with me. We were like brothers, even though he'd gone to public school at six and I'd been shipped off to the North-wood Academy for Boys. He'd been the first boy I'd ever kissed. He was the only person who had listened to me crying because my parents never came to any of my games when I was a young teen and was so fucking confused about life, me, and my need to kiss handsome boys like Apollo. After a few kisses and cuddles, I'd come to the real-ization that Apollo and I weren't meant to be more than best friends. He'd quickly agreed, and we'd grown that much closer. He was my friend, soul brother, cook, personal assistant, and ass-kicker when it was needed, which was pretty much on a daily basis—the ass-kicking, that is.

"So what's wrong?"

I plucked a wedge of carrot from the salad he'd tossed together. The man had serious cooking skills and a wicked-keen way of seeing into me. He spun from his pot, folded his arms over his lean chest, and pinned me to the wall with deep brown eyes.

"I met this guy…"

That brought some light into his eyes. "Oh? Good!" He was always after me to date more and come out. Embrace my inner gay man. Stop trying to impress my parents. Dress better and learn to use the toilet brush, for God's sake.

"Oh, not good." I tossed the carrot into my mouth and chewed. Apollo rolled his eyes. "No, do not do that," I said around the carrot. He turned back to his pot and stirred with a vengeance. "See, when we first ran into each other he was obviously having some sort of episode. Is that soup?"

"Yes, it's celery soup." He threw me a dark look. "And of course, you being Adler, you said something that you thought would be funny but was the exact opposite."

I stared at the wiry man with the undercut and eyebrow piercing. "Maybe."

"You're such a twat," he said as he ladled out two bowls of soup then carried them over to the island. "Here —be careful, it's hot." I cocked an eyebrow at him. "I feel like I have to explain these things to you, because you naturally slip into four-year-old Adler-mode even though you're now six feet two."

"Four," I corrected gently.

"Anything over six feet doesn't matter."

"Not when you're five feet nothing," I commented, then spooned up some creamy soup and blew on it.

"I'm five seven, thank you very much. So, back to you, because you're the one who's the mayor of Fuck-Up-My-Life Land."

"Right, yeah, so I said something stupid to the man and—"

"Is he a hockey player?" Apollo handed me a cloth napkin, then shook his out and placed it over his lap to protect his tight, black skinny jeans.

"No, I think he's a social media guy. Like to help with the whole 'Tennant Rowe and Jared Madsen are butt-sexing each other and want to tell the world about it' situation."

"Mmm, I see. He's a spin doctor?"

"I don't know. 'Social media dude' works. But yeah, he's got these eyes and a mouth…"

"Good to know. Makes seeing and speaking easier."

"Quit being so Apollo, okay? Tell me what to do. How do I make things right with him?" I slurped my soup, made a yummy sound, then chanced a peek at my best and only friend.

"Well, what I'd suggest is not to be a wise-cracking ass-trout when you run into him next. You don't have to entertain people for them to like you, Adler."

"I know." I grabbed some oyster crackers from a small bowl and sprinkled them on top of my soup. "Did I ever mention how glad I am that you decided to come work for me when my mother suggested I get a PA who wears an apron?"

"It was the apron that clinched the deal."

I nudged his shoulder with mine and finished my soup. Maybe the celery would make me less inclined to be an ass-trout.

I SHOULD HAVE KNOWN that celery wouldn't make me less stupid. I mean, if it did have that kind of magical capability, everyone on Earth would be incredibly smart and tinted green from all the celery they consumed.

The next day I rolled through the players' entrance like a man on a mission. I had two goals for morning skate. Show the coach that my being traded there was a good thing, and find the social media guy and apologize for making that bladder and cock crack. Cracks. Two cracks to make amends for.

The Railers dressing room was buzzing with masculine conversation. A sock hit me in the side of the face the moment I stepped foot inside. I threw a dark look at Stan, the Russian goalie who spoke little English but wore Hulk and Pokémon tattoos like prefect badges.

"Ha!" Stan roared, then went back to talking to his equipment like it was completely normal. Goalies are beyond odd.

I made eye contact with Tennant, who might be one of the prettiest men I'd ever met, right after Media Man with the lush mouth and haunted eyes. He nodded, and I did the same.

I'd keep a close eye on his and Madsen coming out. Not that I was crossing that flaming bridge anytime soon. Telling my parents had been bad enough. They hadn't gotten mad. Getting angry would have required caring enough to feel such a powerful emotion. Nope. They'd just mumbled something as they went out the door to work or for cocktails at the country club. It might have been "Okay" or "Great, he's a fag now as well as a hockey player. When will the shame end?" or maybe "When did the Montclairs say they were joining us for skiing in Vale this year?"

AFTER I PEELED my suit off and was in compression shorts and an old Skid Row shirt from their '89 tour, I pulled my cell out of my bag, found my ear buds, and went off in search of a treadmill. I found one next to Arvy. He gave me an easy smile. I decided to tell him a joke about a rabbi and a priest who were buying a car together.

"They decide to store the car at the priest's house. So one day, the rabbi goes over to see the car and finds the priest sprinkling water on it. The rabbi asks, 'What are you doing?' The priest replies, 'I'm blessing the car.' So the rabbi says, 'Okay, since we're doing that...' and takes out a hacksaw and cuts two inches off the tailpipe."

Arvy laughed so hard he fell off his treadmill and had to get the new bruise on his leg iced down. See now, humor *did* work to make people like you, despite what Apollo always said. Feeling pretty good about myself, I plugged my ear buds into my cell and slid the phone into the band on my right bicep. I found my jogging playlist. Lots of Cinderella, Guns N' Roses, some Lita Ford, and a fat dollop of Bon Jovi.

I raised the speed and incline, and ran. There was something about the steady pounding of my feet hitting the belt that worked like a natural high. The stresses of life melted away and I could forget for a minute that I was facing another Christmas with Apollo, while the family— and I use that term loosely, because what I knew about real family could fit on the head of a pin—were off doing anything but seeing me.

"Ah, fuck that crap," I grumbled. I cranked up the tunes and ran until someone slapped my slick back. I threw a look to the left, eyes burning as sweat ran into them. Coach Madsen was standing beside me. I pulled my ear buds out.

"Layton Foxx is looking for you," he said as I slowed my pace and dropped the incline. I took the towel he held up to me.

"Thanks." I scrubbed at my face. "Uh, who's Layton Foxx?" I asked, then peeled my wet T-shirt off so I could run the towel over my chest and stomach.

"He's the crisis management guy, and he wants to talk to you before morning skate. He's in the press room right now."

Oh shit, the media guy with the kissable mouth? He wanted to talk to me? Fuuuuuuck.

"Okay, thanks, Coach." I tossed my shirt around my shoulders and jumped off the treadmill, pulling the cord from my cell phone as I thundered off to find Layton Foxx.

Foxx? Yes, he certainly was. I bet he heard that a lot.

Maybe I could make up something funny to say about him being foxy. Or maybe I'd better not.

I almost missed the press room, and skidded to a halt right in front of the open door as Bob Seger blared out of my cell. Layton Foxx lifted those gorgeous dark gray eyes from the iPad in his hands, and my heartbeat tripled.

THREE

Layton

I couldn't breathe again.

Not just because Adler appeared at my doorway quickly and with no warning, but also because the man was naked. Not entirely naked, of course. He wore tight-fitting shorts, but his shirt was around his shoulders, his skin slicked with sweat, and he looked like he'd run the entire way here from a very long way away.

Breathing was hard because of the shock, plus the fact that I'd honestly never seen anything so perfect as the acres of skin, hard muscles, and that V with the treasure trail vanishing into his shorts. The whole porn-worthy scene was more than I could handle and remain coherent. So I had to try damn hard, which put me off-balance. Adler was my first meeting that morning, but the one I was most worried about given our two previous meetings and the amount of crap the man spoke.

"Hey," he said at the door, and waited.

"Come in," was about all I could muster up to say. "Sit down," I added.

He crossed the threshold, and with his hand on the door handle made a gesture that I assumed was a question whether he should shut the door.

"Shut the door," I confirmed. Okay, so this was going well. Come in, close the door, sit down, and so far he'd done everything I said. He shrugged on his T-shirt, shimmying to get it to fall into place then tugging it down. Through all that, all I could do was watch. There's nothing sexier in my opinion than a man stretching to dress or undress, where glimpses of skin are on display, teasing and suggesting what else there might be. My last lover had got pissed at the time it took for me to undress him, kissing every exposed inch, but that's who I am. I focus hard on tasks in hand to the point of obsession.

And I could spend a lot of time obsessing over the body of the player sitting in the chair opposite me. Shame that jocks had the bodies, and very often the looks, but in my experience a lot had mean, self-obsessed streaks.

Apart from Ten and the others I'd already spoken to the day before; they seemed cool, intelligent, sensible, focused. Whereas Adler was a brainless idiot who liked to talk about genitalia. Shame, because he was gorgeous, and I was still hard from his reverse striptease.

"Adler Lockhart, 62 left wing, I want to apologize," he said in one long sentence, before I could start with my introduction to who I was and what I wanted from the team and mention anything about confidentiality. "It was out of line commenting on your bladder, and cocks in general."

"Okay." It would have been fine if he'd left it there, but no, the man carried on.

"I tend to overtalk, and when I don't know exactly what to say then I come out with all kinds of shit, like commenting on your small bladder. Which I'm sure isn't small. I mean, no man wants to be told they have a small anything, right? I'm sure your bladder is very much in proportion with the rest of your body. And as to the sex thing in the parking garage, well I get uncomfortable debating the various places my teammates stick their cocks, and I don't really want to think of Ten that way. I mean, he's a nice guy, not that I know him really well given that I haven't been with the team long since the trade, but he's a good player. Thinking about his cock isn't something I really want to be doing. Or Coach Madsen's either, to be honest. What they do with each other's cocks in their spare time is up to them." He stopped his speech at that moment and bit his lip, a flush on his cheeks. "Well, shit," he added.

At that moment I could have happily waved away the overtalking and the inappropriate subject matter, signed off on having spoken to him, and been on my way. But that wasn't my job, and I took a moment to look down at the paperwork in front of me.

"I think you would benefit from some sensitivity training," I began.

"Hell no. I'm sensitive. I can be sensitive."

"It's standard procedure," I reassured him and lied at the same time.

"Oh." He deflated a little. "You mean everyone has to do it?"

I wish at that moment I'd just said yes, because that would have stopped Adler in his tracks. But no, I had to be all cagey. "That's confidential."

He frowned. "So not everyone, then."

"Like I said, confidential."

"What about Arvy?"

I couldn't for the life of me think why he was picking

on Arvy as an example, so I missed another opportunity to cut this dead. "Confidential," I said.

"I see, so he has this gay cousin, which gives him an out from an entire day wasted listening to shit about what I can and can't say?"

"Mr. Lockhart—"

"So if you know someone who knows someone, then you have an out. Right?"

"That's not how it works—"

"I know Arvy," he said, and sat back in his chair. "I have to think about what I say in front of him, so that's me being sensitive."

"You're missing the point," I began patiently, and then I really screwed the pooch. "Wait, Arvy was there when you were handling your junk in the parking lot."

"Oh," Adler said and sighed noisily. Then he scrubbed his eyes with his fingers. "Hate that political correctness shit," he muttered.

I assumed he meant the sensitivity training, but I wanted to move on from this. "It's all common sense, and with the changes on the team it's vital we present a united front to any and all media inquiries."

"Hell, I don't care what Ten and the coach do." He looked at me, and I waited for more, because he seemed like he was going to add to that sentence. Only he didn't. His lips thinned like he was trying very hard to hold something back.

I took that as a sign that he was about to say something crass, and almost felt proud that he'd held back. I looked down at my sketched notes.

"This is a question you don't need to answer, but it would be helpful to know if you have any religious objections to the situation that we should make a note of."

"Christ, no," he said, then snorted a laugh at his own joke. He quickly stopped and schooled his face into all serious business. "Sorry, couldn't stop myself."

And that is your problem, Mr. Hockey Guy.

I mentally crossed through religion; put an extra tick in the sensitivity training column because this guy seriously had no filter.

"Do you have any questions for me?" I asked, attempting to bring the mercifully short meeting to an end.

"That's it?" he asked, and looked surprised.

"This was just to touch base, get to know the team sort of thing."

Adler crossed his arms over his chest again, and I saw the muscles bunch; this man was strong. "You don't want to ask any questions about me?"

"We'll talk at length later, post sensitivity training."

"Honestly no more questions?"

"No. My primary focus is building a social media presence that supports the team as a whole and has the face of equality."

He nodded slowly. "So you mean to the outside we're all fucking happy-clappy praise be to the sexual alphabet in all its iterations?"

I wanted to say that was why he needed training on what was appropriate. I didn't.

"This is an explosive situation, Mr. Lockhart. The Railers could make a really positive mark here."

"Will you quit calling me that? My name is Adler, or Ad, or Adzee if you want to go the whole hockey nickname route adding zee on the end of every last name. Which would make you Foxxzee, which is cool."

I ignored that. "Adler, you may not understand the situation in full, but this is the first NHL player making a strong statement about who he is so that he can live openly with his partner."

"I get it," he said defensively. "I'm not fucking stupid, I just don't get why it has to be a thing."

He looked genuinely puzzled, a typical example of someone who has never had to fight for recognition. I bet he'd never been beaten on for his identity in any way, bet he'd never had a day of fear. I wanted so much to say all that, but this wasn't the forum for that type of discussion. It was a preliminary meeting, and nothing to do with countering ignorance. It was about a baseline, about a quick face-to-face with every player to see what work I needed to do to present a united front as a team. Education, awareness, sensitivity—that was what this was about.

"THANK YOU FOR COMING IN," I began, but he waved the words away.

"Love is love, right? I mean, I've never been in love with a man, have you?"

Wait up. Where did that come from? Isn't he contradicting himself there? One minute he's saying love is love, and then he picks up on loving a man.

"The first session is tomorrow after morning skate," I announced, ignoring what he'd said.

He looked frustrated. "I don't get this," he snapped. "Why it's even a thing. Hell, it's worse that a player is fucking a coach than that it's two men."

Okay, none of what he was saying was making sense now, and I really needed him out of this small office space, because, hell, this impassioned, nearly angry man was making me feel incredibly uncomfortable. I stood up and shuffled around the desk, opening the door.

"Thank you," I said, hoping he'd get the hint.

He stood up and faced me, far too close for comfort, and I could see his expression had changed from confused to utterly focused. He moved to the door, but instead of walking out he leaned on it until it closed and we were both inside.

I didn't like this; I could feel my chest tightening. No one had said that Adler Lockhart was the sort of man to intimidate, but hell, I felt like I was back in school.

"You missed off one vital question on your list," he said, his hands on his hips, his large frame completely blocking the only exit from the room.

Pushing through the rushing noise in my head, I stepped back a little until my ass hit the desk. I rested my hands behind me, feeling for the stapler. It wasn't big, but it was enough to make my fist a weapon.

"What was that?" I asked, waiting for the vitriol and the flash of violence.

"You never asked how I identify myself; you need to add that to your list before you push people into training about how to be fucking sensitive to a sexual orientation situation. Then you need to say something about it not leaving this room."

"The training will cover—"

"Ask me now," he interrupted, his hands dropping from his hips and hanging loose at his sides. They weren't fists, he wasn't tight with anger, and he was literally requesting that I give him the question. "Go on," he continued. "Say, 'Adler Lockhart, who do you like to sleep with in your spare time?' and see what I say."

"This is ridiculous," I snapped. "You need to leave." His body posture screamed relaxed and teasing, but his challenge scared me.

"Ask me."

I just wanted him out of the room. I was confused and

stressed and he was digging for something from me, God knew what. "For goodness sake. What is your sexual orientation?"

He nodded then, and pushed himself away from the door.

"I'm gay," he announced.

I didn't believe him, "You can go," I said, and tensed in anger. This wasn't him trying to assert authority or intimidate me; this was a huge fucking wind-up.

"No, I'm serious. I fuck guys, or they fuck me—mostly I fuck them. So I don't need the political correctness training. And you can't tell anyone that, because I'm not even out to the team."

I looked at him and saw how earnest he appeared. The man was actually gay? Hell, if he was saying it to get out of the training, he needed to understand that words and lies hurt.

"Right?" he asked. "I can skip the training."

Did he actually believe he wasn't a walking disaster with a mouth that spewed garbage? Him saying he was gay? That didn't mean a thing, although if he was telling the truth, then I needed to rethink the typical questions I should ask in the baseline assessment.

"You can go," I repeated.

"But I said—"

"I'll see you tomorrow at the session. All the information is posted on the board in the locker room."

He sighed noisily and opened the door. But my relief was short-lived when he didn't leave but hovered there in the open doorway. "I think it's cool to see a couple like Ten and Coach who don't seem to self-destruct after a few months. I hope they're very happy, and I'll attend the training so you can tick your boxes, but I won't like it."

He left then, closing the door behind him.

As soon as the door shut, I could feel the tension in my body leach out a little at a time as I attempted to sort through the feelings inside me.

Was it bad that once the fear subsided, in its place there was honest-to-goodness arousal? Was it wrong to feel a hundred kinds of confused about the man who'd just left?

Thankfully, next up was this big Russian called Stanislav Lyamin.

"Call Stan," he said, and extended his big, meaty hand. I shook it, and he had a grip of iron. He also had a wide grin, soft dopey eyes, and a tattoo on his biceps of a yellow figure I could swear was a Pokémon. Interesting.

"Do we need a translator?" I asked in English. Not that I could have asked that in Russian. He stared at me blankly, and I opened up my phone and searched for Google Translate. I typed in "Do you need a translator?" and it returned "Вам нужен переводчик?" Which I could show him, or maybe I could use the phonetic-type thing under it. "Vam nuzhen perevodchik?" I asked.

He looked at me blankly again, and then just as I was considering phoning management and asking for a translator, he snorted a laugh.

"English good," he said, giving me a lot of doubt about exactly how good his English was.

I cleared my throat, assumed Stan was what he wanted to be called, and played the delaying tactic of taking a long pull of my cooling coffee.

"Caffeine bad," Stan said, then picked up the Snickers on my desk. He wrinkled his nose at it, then stared at me. "Lunch?" he asked, and dropped the offending chocolate bar back onto my paperwork.

Yep, a snickers and coffee was my lunch, but that was

only because I didn't have time to stop today. Chocolate plus caffeine equaled energy, which was what I needed.

"Yes."

"Eat is shit, da?" he asked.

"Da," I said, then shrugged in that "What can I do?" kind of way.

He frowned at me and leaned forward, and I braced myself for more Russian commentary. He said nothing.

"Okay," I said, readying what I wanted to say next and clearing words from Google Translate.

"Okay," Stan repeated cheerfully, stood up, and left the office, closing the door behind him.

Oh. That went well. Guess I really did need a translator.

Someone knocked on the door.

"Come in," I called, and the door opened. Yet another big hockey player stood there looking like he'd rather be anywhere else.

Well, me too. I wasn't sure I could handle another session in this small room with the door shut—not when the remnants of a tight anxiety refused to leave me.

I'm a professional. I can do this.

"Hi." I extended a hand.

The player shook it but let go. "Dieter Lehmann," he began, and seemed nervous. "My jersey number is 56, I play left wing," He stopped and seemed to gather his thoughts, because the nerves slipped away and abruptly he was all confidence, "I'm kind of an all-around sex god."

I loved the way hockey players identified themselves by name, position and number. The sex god part was a bit worrying, though. I looked at him steadily, but he didn't retract the sex god thing. Great. He looked a little pale, and tired, but knowing a jock he'd probably been up all night partying. I really had my job cut out here.

"Have a seat, Dieter."

Dieter sat, and wriggled in the chair like he wasn't comfortable. Finally he looked up at me, and I saw that confidence hadn't slipped.

"Before we start," he began, "I have the number 56 now, but if your records show me having 69 on my jersey in college, then you know it was only a joke. Right?"

I nodded but inwardly groaned. This was going to be a long day.

FOUR

Adler

The fucker didn't believe me.

That bounced around inside my head all during morning skate. How could he not believe me? I mean, come on, right? I tell the guy I'm gay and he looks at me like I'm the biggest liar in the world, then throws me out like a burger teeming with botulism. It wasn't like I told people I was gay all the time. Apollo knew, but he was my brother from another mother... and father. Just Cole and Karrie Anne knew, and now Layton Foxx. None of them, aside from Apollo, had given two shits. How can you not give a damn about something as important as that?

"Is there a reason you're standing there?"

I gave Coach Madsen a confused look.

"Offensive drills are done. This is a defensive meeting."

I looked around and saw only defensive players staring at me.

"Oh right, yeah, I knew that. I was just wondering if anyone had seen that movie with the guy and that girl? No? Pity. It's really good. Things blow up. I'll just go now."

Adler, you are a moron.

One of the equipment managers slid some guards onto my blades, and I thumped off, face red, stomach all sorts of knotted up, my goal the dressing room. Honestly. It had been my plan to shower and go home to talk to Apollo. Then I'd eat, come back to the barn, and go out there and beat the sass out of Philadelphia. But then I saw Layton Foxx in that tiny room, and all my plans went left of center. I stopped on a dime, took a step in reverse, and walked into the press room. His head came up and his eyes—they were incredible stormy gray eyes with thick, dark lashes—flared when he saw me. He grabbed the stapler.

"Okay, see here's the thing…" I used my stick to shut the door. "I don't think you get how hard it was for me to tell you that I'm gay."

"I really wish you'd open the door." He held on to that stapler like it was a Ruger or something. "We're done for the day."

"Yeah, I thought so too, but how you treated me is stuck in my chest." I thumped on my breastbone with a gloved hand.

Layton eyed me nervously. He was so damn enticing in an uptight, corporate way. He needed me to peel him out of that spiffy suit, lay him over that ugly desk, and make love to him until he was loose as a damn goose. I bet he bottomed. I hoped he did. Also, he needed to let go of that stapler.

"Are you going to shoot me in the eye with a staple or something?"

"What? No." He put the stapler down but left a well-manicured hand resting on it. He had nice fingers. Soft looking, like he never did dirty work or tinkered with engines. Not that I tinkered with engines either, but my hands looked like hockey player hands. Scarred up from fights and being slashed by opposing players. "You need to go, though."

No, what I need to do is reach down and adjust my cock, Foxx. Christ, but your surname fits you.

"I think you should at least acknowledge how tough it was for me to tell you my sexual orientation."

He studied me for a long moment, his fingers slipping from the stapler to rest on his piles of papers and forms.

"So can you cough something out, or not?"

"I understand how hard that must have been for you."

"Thank you."

I turned, opened the door, and went to the dressing room more confused than I had been before I'd intimidated Foxx into saying what I wanted. Shit. Now I felt like a dick. A dick with a boner. A double dick. I couldn't shower until the fucking thing went down. The morning was officially a train wreck for the newest addition to the Railers team. I snorted at my own joke, then sat down to will my erection away.

———

"SEE, this is why I don't allow you on Twitter," Apollo huffed as he flung a plate of broiled chicken, asparagus and wild rice in front of me. "You have no filter. You just feel and talk. I blame it on Cole and Karrie Anne. If they'd actually spent some quality time with you when you were a kid, you wouldn't feel this need to be rude and loud just to get attention."

"I'm not rude," I muttered, then began cutting my chicken breast into strips.

"Oh yes you are. You don't mean to be, but you are. Cut that into smaller bites. I know my mother raised you better," he sniffed before sitting down beside me at the island in my kitchen.

"I just wanted some fucking validation—is that so bad?"

"No, it's not, but you need that from your parents and not some stranger." He poured me some water, then gently put the glass by my plate.

"I'll have better luck getting it from a stranger."

"Oh Adler, shit, man." He draped an arm around my shoulders as I chewed on his perfectly prepared chicken. It was tender and delicious and I'd yet again fucked everything up. Swallowing was hard for a moment.

"So how do I fix it?" I asked after getting the ball of chicken to go down. "The man looked terrified of me."

"You *are* pretty intimidating with all your pads on and waving a stick around."

"I can't make myself smaller," I mumbled, and ate in silence while Apollo tossed out about forty ideas of how to make things better with Layton Foxx. None of them would work in practical application. Could you see me giving the man a nice pen set as an apology? Really? Would that work? Hmm. Maybe… He seemed like the kind of guy who'd get into pens. And staplers. Oh yeah, a new stapler. That would be good, yes? Sure it would. Well, maybe not. Maybe office products that could double as weapons were something I shouldn't give him. I'd buy him a new pen on the way to the barn and present it to him tomorrow after skate when I was being made into a more politically correct hockey player. And he thought I couldn't be sensitive. Pfft.

"DID you know that everyone on your team hates you?" I asked the Philly winger who was nudging me around. "Seriously, they do. I heard them."

"Whatever, Lockhart. How are things at Hogwarts?"

"Ah, I see what you did there. No one has ever commented about my last name and Gilderoy Lockhart before." I rolled my eyes and leaned in to him as the centers lined up for a faceoff. "See, that's why your teammates hate you. It's because of bad chirps like that."

The puck hit the ice. My center shoved it to me, and I flipped it over to one of our defensemen, who took off like a shot but ended up being knocked off his skates by one of the aggressive Philly wingers. That prompted a rebuttal from one of the Railers, who got a penalty call for roughing.

I skated off to catch my breath and wait for the first penalty kill unit to do their thing. Arvy sat next to me, flapping his gums about Philly and how they always worked the boards so damn well, did I have anything cooking after the game, and had I started my Christmas shopping, because he'd seen the bag from the office supply shop and wondered if his mother would like something similar.

"Yeah, they're tough on the boards. No, it's not a Christmas gift. Everyone likes pens."

There, that should shut him up.

"You bought someone pens? Like a bag of Bics?"

Or not…

"No, man, not a bag of Bics. I got him a Montblanc set," I told him as I tried to stay focused on the game.

"Him? Oh, you got pens for your father?"

"I got—what?" That brought me back to Arvy. I tugged off my helmet and waved at an equipment manager for a towel. "Sure, yeah, for my dad."

I'd better pay closer attention to what was being said to

me on the bench. I'd already gotten my ass chewed by Coach for showing up late. It wasn't my fault that the dinky office supply store here didn't have a Cartier boutique. I'd had to linger around while the dude in the dinky store called around to locate the nearest Cartier boutique— which was out in King of Prussia—and have them deliver it by hand to the Harrisburg store. That had tacked on another couple of hundred bucks to the sum, but so what? When you're paying close to six hundred dollars for a pen and a leather business card holder, what's another two hundred and fifty? It was a drop in the cash bucket for a Lockhart. Waiting had set me back over two hours, and I'd arrived at the game with just enough time to tape up and lace up. Hence the chewing out from the head coach. Foxxy man had better appreciate the gift.

"Let's roll," the associate coach barked over my head. I scrubbed my face, then threw the towel onto the bench. Slapping my helmet on, I tossed a leg over the boards and waited for the first penalty kill unit to come back. As soon as one man was off, I hit the ice, skating up to one of the Philly wingers and lifting his stick to steal the puck.

Someone shouted at me. I glanced across the neutral zone to see Tennant Rowe, who should have gone off, wide open. I shuttled the puck to him and we made a beeline for the Philadelphia end of the ice. The goalie dropped down, his dark eyes flicking back and forth as Rowe and I raced at him. The crowd was up and on its feet. Tennant passed to me, I passed back to Ten, and the Philadelphia goalie knew he was in trouble.

The pass from Rowe was a perfect tape-to-tape right in front of the Philly net. The goalie tried his best. He stretched out as the puck sailed in front of him, trying to poke check the puck away, but Rowe was demonically good at passing. The puck bounced off my skate right to my waiting stick, and I flicked it up and over the goalie as he scrambled to get back into his crease. Shaking twine. Red light. Thunderously happy Railers' fans. Now that was sweet. A shorthanded goal as my first point as a Railer. Hoped my old team back in Columbus saw that on the highlight reels and maybe had second thoughts about trading me.

Rowe and the other two Railers on the ice mobbed me. I skated to my bench and got twenty-something knuckle bumps and the puck for my collection. All in all, a damn fine play that led into a solid outing. Beating Philly always felt good.

Coach Madsen slapped my shoulder, then Arvy patted my helmet. I scanned the crowd for Apollo. He'd be out there, leaping around while wearing one of my sweaters. At least *someone* was there to cheer for me…

FIVE

Layton

I never meant to go to the game, even though being the professional I am meant that I should really learn more about the sport. I'd decided early on that after the ups and downs of the first two days, I should just go home and chill out.

Then I got a text from David; my brother had this incredible way with words. "Mom said she'd call you tonight."

Great. A call from my mom would arrive at precisely eight p.m.; she was nothing if not a creature of habit. Why did we need to talk again so soon? We'd only spoken the night before, and I'd listened to her reel off the news about each of my siblings, their wives, and the assorted grandchildren. Had I done something wrong? I couldn't imagine what it had been. Last time she'd got pissed at me was when I'd announced I wasn't moving home, time before that it had been because I hadn't told her I was gay as soon as I knew.

Like *that* would have been an easy conversation. If I recall right, it was an announcement I made in between

David telling us that his wife, Cindy, was pregnant again, and Louise starting a round-table fight about condoms.

When I'd blurted out what I wanted to say to my family at the scarred kitchen table, I remember the smack upside my head from Mom. She said she'd known—as had all of my siblings, come to think of it—but then she proceeded to question me about why I'd made it into such a big thing.

Well, fuck. Announcing I was gay *had* been a big thing that I'd angsted over for months.

Which brought Adler Lockhart and his scary presence into my head, and that was another reason I wanted to avoid the game. That man shook me, and I don't mean just because of the fact that he was a big guy, a jock, and he intimidated me. No, this was more than that.

He'd slumped a little coming into the room—trying to make himself look smaller, I thought.

And then he'd demanded that I acknowledge how hard it had been for him to admit he was gay, and what could I say?

MY FAMILY WAS FAR *from judgmental, moving from shock to riding my ass about fashion and condoms every time we talked thereafter. In my heart I'd known they wouldn't care, not about who I chose to sleep with, or fall in love with, but they would worry about the challenges I faced. That was just the way my family worked.*

I reassured them that I would get my degree and I could look after myself. David stared at me like I'd grown a second head, and Zach nudged him, and I'd tensed; I remember that.

"You don't need a degree, or to leave. You know you can always work with me," David mumbled. "Electrician, it's a good trade."

"Or with me—plumbing, family business," Zach added.

"I'll be okay."

I had my entire college life mapped out, worked three jobs, saved every penny, had a scholarship to NYU, and I knew what I wanted to do when I finished. I wanted to have a career I could shape myself, get a good apartment, a boyfriend, live a different life to my siblings, who'd all settled in the same town they'd been born in.

And I wanted to escape the shame I felt looking at my siblings, knowing what they knew about me, what they'd seen, how they'd helped to patch up the wounds scraped into my soul.

"You'll be alone, though," Zach said, but he couldn't quite meet my gaze, and I knew why. They all thought I was too damaged to ever get over what had happened. But what nobody in my family realized was that it didn't matter whether I got over it—I would live my life and wouldn't let fear stop me.

And I really wanted out of this town, with the nightmares that chased me around every corner. People here knew about me, and I hated it. I craved the anonymity of a big city. Craved it like it was heroin and I was an addict.

Mom summed up the feeling at the table. "We're always here for you," she murmured, and somehow in that simple sentence she made everything right in the world. Until she started to nag about dangers and not telling her and, yeah, it deteriorated after that, back to Mom thinking I should move back home after college and that cities weren't safe.

I didn't argue with them, but I disagreed. The city was open and secure and I could be myself. I could get a boyfriend, and drink fancy coffees, and wear a suit, and be the first person in my family to go to college and get a degree.

AGAIN, Adler was there in my thoughts.

He didn't have that luxury, nor did Ten, and I needed to know more about the toxic environment in hockey that potentially judged a man on the sort of relationship he wanted. Seemed to me from some of the conversations I'd had that it was a problem bigger than "hating on the gays," as Dieter had so colorfully put it. That had been after I'd suggested that any shade of sexual innuendo was a bad one. He'd looked really uncomfortable, then brightened as he quickly apologized for the 69 on his jersey again.

Head meet desk.

So I hadn't gone home as planned, and I was watching the game, mostly to avoid having to talk to my mom. I had a pass to sit in the press box, or at least perch on the edge of a chair in the corner and not take up much space. Management had assigned Jane to give me some insight on the game, and I made notes. Copious amounts of scribbles that I hoped would make sense when I looked at them later.

"Each game has three periods," she began, and I couldn't help asking questions about that, a mess of whys and whens that ended with her all confused over what to explain first.

"Sorry," I apologized when she stopped talking and frowned.

Her frown eased, "No, don't be. It's difficult to get a handle on things if you've never watched a game before. I get it."

"Is that what you were like?" I asked, hoping I would have a friend in ignorance.

"Me? No, my dad and granddad were both players, and my dad is a coach, so I was brought up in a hockey family."

I looked down at my notes, "So, PK and PP are something different?"

She explained something that sounded like a math equation, and I dutifully wrote it all down.

"Some penalties are two minutes," she said, "some five,

some have both, or more, sometimes the player will..." She stopped and shook her head. "Tell you what, let's watch the game and just experience it for real."

I nodded, because my head was spinning, and while I waited for her to get drinks I ordered *Hockey for Dummies* from Amazon, paying extra for next day delivery. Maybe the rules that guided this game were the reason for the hyper-masculinity I'd sensed in the day's short meetings. I knew hockey players fought; maybe the perception was that if you were gay you weren't able to fight? Should I start with the concept that players accepted and perpetu-ated stereotypes as normal?

I thought about Adler. Damn man had got into my thoughts again. He was a stereotypical bad guy, or at least how I perceived a bad guy, even though there was a soft-ness in his eyes. He'd worked hard to become what he needed to be. In doing that, he'd had to hide the real him, the same as Ten. I made some extra notes about other sports to research. Arvy had mentioned in his meeting that one of the slurs he'd heard was a hockey player being called a figure skater. I assumed the implication there was that figure skating wasn't hard or something, or maybe it was too flamboyant. I made a note of that to follow up on. Maybe the guys on the team needed a bonding day with a figure skater to see that it was hard work, which I assumed it was.

When Jane got back with two coffees and her trade-mark smile, there were skaters on the ice, but they weren't doing anything dramatic. They were lining up, mostly—well, five of them from each team, the rest of the guys on separate benches. The Railers were in a dusky blue, and the visiting team in orange. The national anthem played over the sound system, and I considered what the guys on the team—the Norwegians, Germans, Russians, and more than a couple of Canadians—thought of the national anthem being the American one. Did that cause any friction? Was that a core issue as well?

Jeez, my mind was racing.

"The skaters out there now are what they call the first line," Jane explained. "Three forwards, two defense, and obviously the goalie."

"Stan."

"Yep."

I mentally fist-pumped that I had at least one name right. "And is Ten on the ice to start?"

"No, he's our second line center, with Lockhart and Lehmann on his wings—he'll be on when they change."

Something shifted inside me at the mention of Adler's name. Stupid.

The clock on the Jumbotron showed 20:00, and then the puck dropped and I didn't have a second to make any more notes. The changes were all over the place, men jumping the boards in a rhythm that made no sense to me at first, the numbers on their jerseys a blur as the puck moved up and down the ice.

Well, I say it moved. I couldn't actually see it. In fact it took an entire two periods before I realized I was trying to track the wrong thing and needed to look at the bigger picture. The Railers scored twice in that second period, but the Flyers scored one, so going into the last period it was like the entire crowd of supporters in blue were on their feet every time the Railers had the puck.

Ten was fast. He hadn't scored a goal, but he'd got an assist, which was a good thing, apparently. But boy, he skated rings around the other team, and I couldn't help but think the speed, skill, and absolute confidence were sexy.

And there was Adler, coming over the boards and… wait, there was confusion. Hadn't Ten been out just finishing a power play or something? Ten had the puck, he passed to Adler, there was some fancy moving about, and then the entire stadium erupted as Adler shot the puck into the net.

The goal horn sounded, the East River Arena in chaos, and I didn't even think about it—I was on my feet next to Jane and cheering for the Railers.

For Adler.

Damn man.

I watched him hug Ten and the others on the ice, then fist-bump his teammates. The mood in the arena changed, the fans chanting for Stan over and over, like everyone could feel a win.

The last few minutes passed in a blur of fighting and tired men, and no more goals.

We'd won. The Railers all lined up and did these cool head-bumps with Stan, and then they all skated off the ice, the crowd still cheering.

"This way," Jane said, and took my elbow to guide me out of the press room, down convoluted corridors, ending up outside the locker rooms. "This is media availability," she explained, and ushered me in.

Right into the start of what looked like a porn movie.

Okay, so no one was naked, in fact a lot of the players wore thin shirts, and some were still in full uniform. But Adler wasn't. He was bare-chested and back down to those skinny shorts already. And he was being interviewed.

I was shoved forward, I guess so I could experience the post-game interview, but that put me way too close to Adler, who caught my eye and held my gaze as he answered a question about a shorthanded goal, whatever that was. Something passed between us, an acknowledgment of sorts, and I watched as he blinked, my chest tight. I didn't understand what had just happened. Maybe it was just a way of me saying that I believed what he'd told me and that I would hold his secrets.

"Talk us through the goal," one woman asked, thrusting a microphone in front of him and waggling it under his nose. He was hemmed in, ten people around him, all with microphones or recording devices, and I knew I wouldn't be able to handle that. He began talking about the technical side of the goal, and there was nodding in the small group, and some congratulations. He held up a puck, and a couple of them took photos. He was slick with sweat, a towel around his neck, and he looked so relaxed and happy.

"How did you feel about the goal?" someone asked.

He looked at me again as he answered the last question. "Awesome," he said.

I couldn't help it, I smiled at him, his joy and excitement infectious, and he grinned back. Someone shoved me from behind, not deliberately, but I tensed, and the smile dropped from my face.

I turned and walked away.

But not before I'd seen the flash of some weird expression on Adler's face. Concern, maybe?

Last thing I needed was someone worrying about my hang-ups, and anyway, by the time I was back in the small office space with my notebook, I was absolutely fine. I pulled out a fresh notebook and began transcribing the scribbled notes into order. I headed everything accordingly —observations, outcomes, conclusions, and an area for possible research. Figure Skater. Endemic gender bias. And something else I needed to add, but I couldn't make it out in my notes.

When I realized what I'd written, I deliberately closed the rough notes and slid the book into my drawer.

Adler Lockhart, 62, second line, summer-sky eyes.

BY THE TIME I left the office, it seemed like East River just held staff and some players. The parking garage that was assigned to staff was half full, and all I really wanted was to get into my car and go home. I spotted Adler before he saw me; he was standing by a gorgeous silver sports car, one of many down here. Actually, you could tell which cars belonged to players; they were shiny and low and sported logos like Porsche or Ferrari, either that or they were huge SUV monstrosities. .

I braced myself to talk to Adler, but when I got nearer I saw he was talking to someone, and I took a detour to get to my car. The conversation they were having seemed deep, and the other person, a dark-skinned man sporting a Railers jersey, had his hands crossed over his chest and appeared to be listening to Adler intently.

Was he Adler's boyfriend? They were standing very close to each other, and when Adler pulled the guy in for a hug, I guessed I was right. Then I glanced around the parking area. What if someone walked out and saw them? I thought Adler wanted to keep his secret.

They climbed into the car, and I stood in the shadows near my own car until they left. Jumping into my car, I drove home, and resolved to mention to Adler that secrets didn't stay hidden if you went around hugging your boyfriend in plain view.

I certainly didn't think about the look we'd exchanged or the unidentifiable *thing* that had loosened in my chest.

Not at all.

SIX

Adler

I woke up feeling great. I'd scored the game-winning goal last night. Apollo and I had played a wickedly badass round of some zombie first-person shooter game on the Xbox before bed and I'd whipped him like a soufflé. Do you whip soufflés? Whatever. He'd got turned into a mindless zombie and I hadn't, so go Adler.

Layton and I had made eye contact, and there had been something… tender or caring in his look. I'd dreamed about touching his face and kissing his spine all the way down to his pert ass.

Hoping to continue the good vibes into a new day, I jumped out of bed, beat off in the shower, because spine-kissing fantasy, ate the plate of eggs and bacon Apollo put in front of me before I was made to comment on what kind of holiday window cling he should put on the sliding glass doors. I didn't care, because no one would see them and I'd ignore them. He could put window clings of naked Layton Foxx up there and…

I paused and glanced at the icy sliders. If naked Layton Foxx were a window cling, I'd notice. Hell, I'd be over there tonguing the damn frosty glass. Shit, my dick was already noticing. That man was turning me into a six-foot-four walking erection. I checked on the nicely wrapped pen set in my duffel, pulled a coat on over my suit jacket, and made my way to the barn.

Listening to Cinderella as I poked along in early morning Harrisburg traffic, I ran over a few scenarios about the gift-giving in our scheduled sensitivity meeting after morning skate. I practiced several lines, but none of them sounded convincing, so I opted just to wing it. What could go wrong? I mean, come on. I was giving the man a Montblanc pen set. Maybe he'd be so grateful and awed by my gift that he'd allow me to give him that blowjob I'd secretly daydreamed about the night before while trying to fall asleep. Bet those gray eyes of his darkened like a thunderhead when he was being loved well.

"Ah man, come on," I growled at my dick as it stiffened yet again. Great. Fucking dicks. I drove around the parking lot of the stadium until my boner went away.

Morning skate took forever. Rowe was all over me the minute I returned to the dressing room after skate, jabbering away about feeling that my addition to the team was obviously a good one, how sweet he and I skated together, and how he and Coach Madsen had set up their Christmas tree last night.

"First Christmas together," Ten said as a peachy-pink blush colored his face. My coloring went from lost-what-little-tan-he-had white to jealous shamrock-green. I excused myself, claiming I had to use the bathroom because of a bad breakfast burrito I'd bought at the gas station coming in. Envy was a nasty emotion. I disliked being jealous, but it was a familiar feeling. I'd spent my childhood being jealous of the time my parents spent at work as well as on their hobbies, traveling, friends. Apollo's relationship with his mother and father. Even the Wright Brothers, because they'd been the ones who'd discovered how to get people off the ground. So yeah, I'd grown up being jealous of airplanes because my parents, Cole and Karrie Anne, spent more time with their jet and personal pilot than they did with me.

Ugh. I had to stop. "Think happy thoughts," I told myself as I snuck back into the changing area.

A fast strip and shower, fingers through the hair, and a quick check on the tie. Package wrapped in silver foil with a blue bow in hand, I jogged past the weight room. I jammed the gift inside my suit jacket. The door to the small office Foxx had been given was open, so I rushed in before anyone could see me and flung the door closed. Layton looked less bug-eyed upon seeing me barge into his space this time. I worked on pulling my shoulders in so that I didn't take up so much room in the cramped area.

"You're early," Layton said. He looked outstanding today. The dark-gray pinstripe fitted him well, showing off his broad shoulders. On his lapel was a rainbow flag pin. "Glad to see you're so enthusiastic about bettering your social interaction skills."

"Right, yeah, totally on that. So, here." I pulled the package out from under my jacket. Layton's slate-toned eyes widened. I shook the gift at him. "This is for you."

"Christmas is three weeks away," he murmured as he eyed the present like it might blow up in his face or something. "And I'm not sure you and I should be exchanging—"

"It's not a Christmas gift. It's an apology gift." I shoved the set at him. He drew back. Okay, he seriously thought it was an incendiary device. Why else would he not take it?

"That wasn't necessary."

"It was." I laid the box on his desk, right beside that

stapler he always seemed to have close at hand. He looked up at me. I stared at him… at his eyes… losing myself and my train of thought as I watched timidity and desire swirling in those pewter depths. I sat down to make myself less intimidating. "Open it."

"Mr. Lockhart…"

"Adler, Mr. Lockhart is my father. Well," I let my gaze touch his firm jaw," that's not what I call my father. He's Cole to me. Like mom is Karrie Anne. That's how my gifts and the checks are always signed. Cards, too. 'Love, Cole and Karrie Anne Lockhart.' Funny, huh?"

"Well I…"

"I mean, the gifts are always top-notch, so it's not like they're cheap gifts. I wish you'd open that and see how sorry I am." I reached over the desk to nudge the nicely wrapped box through papers and notes.

"You didn't need to buy me anything. Just a heartfelt apology works."

"That's an apology from the Cartier boutique." Was there a reason he wasn't getting it? Love comes in boxes from Cartier, Tiffany, or Van Cleef & Arpels. Everyone knows that.

"I can't accept such an expensive gift, Adler. But thank you." He pushed the box back at me. My mind scrambled to make sense of this. "Maybe we should start talking about how some words can be misconstrued when used in—"

I got to my feet. He did as well. Okay, that was fine. He looked good standing. Sitting, too. Lying under me in bed as well, I'd wager.

"I don't get it. This is me trying to make you happy. This isn't a dumb little gift from K-Mart or something. I spent hours getting this for you yesterday. I was almost late for the game because they had to courier this set from

King of Prussia to Harrisburg. That's a lot of thoughtfulness being put into an apology, Foxx. The least you could do is take the damn thing."

His nice jaw jutted out. Ah, well, now he was showing some fire. It made him even more attractive, to be honest. I'd bet he was a lively bottom once he got past being so meek, because there was obviously fire in the man's breast.

"I think I told you that I couldn't accept it." He folded his arms over his chest as his gaze found mine and locked with it. "I'm sorry you got into trouble because of it, but that's not my fault. Now can you sit back down so we can begin work on your sensitivity training?"

"I'm being all kinds of sensitive!" I barked.

He cocked a dark eyebrow.

"What? You think spending hours playing a gem drop game while the perfect pen set for the man you fantasize spine-kissing is *en route* to me isn't sensitive?"

"What?" He coughed. I blinked. "What did you say?" His brows tangled.

"That I spent hours playing some stupid gem drop game on my phone while I waited for the courier to arrive from King of—"

"No, not that. The other part of your comment." He looked flushed and hot. Well, he was always hot, but hot under the collar, I meant.

"I don't know what I said."

His mouth opened and shut a few times. Nothing came out.

"Are you having a seizure or something?" I enquired as he worked to speak or breathe. Wasn't sure which. Maybe he'd need mouth to mouth. I could get into that.

"That's why you need to learn not to feel and speak simultaneously," he finally said.

"Apollo said the same thing in the parking garage last

night. Actually, he says that to me all the time," I commented.

Layton's face tightened. "That's another thing we need to discuss. If you're not out yet, then public displays of affection with your boyfriend in public places shouldn't be happening."

"You said public twice," I pointed out. That seemed to add to his flustered thoughts, which amped up his hotness into the stratosphere. "Were you spying on me?"

"Don't be asinine." He stalked to the door and whipped it open. "This meeting is over. We're out of time, and you're obviously out of touch with how to conduct yourself."

"That's a Hall & Oates song." I couldn't stop looking at his mouth. "And that guy I hugged in the parking lot wasn't my boyfriend—he's my best friend and personal assistant."

"Oh. Maybe you should make sure my advice about public displays is carried home to your boyfriend."

I took a step closer to him. He stood his ground. I pushed the door closed. He straightened his spine and wet his lips. A jolt of lust hit me right in the balls. I wanted to wet his lips for him.

"'Out of Time' is a Hall & Oates song," I told him as the magnetic pull of Layton Foxx had me moving toward him. "And I don't have a boyfriend. You want the job?"

"Hall & Oates is… what?" He took a step in reverse, then faltered, as if he suddenly remembered he wasn't going to be intimidated by me any longer. The cloud of lust and male pheromones was thick on the air. His cologne and mine intermingled and created a new aroma that was rich, sinful and lusty.

"I could use a man in my life to keep my mouth from getting away from me," I said in a gruff voice. His gray eyes darted to my mouth. He wet his lips again. I leaned in slowly, trying to give him time to duck away or skitter to a corner or grab that fucking stapler and staple me in the forehead. He didn't do any of those things, though.

He exhaled shakily through slightly parted lips as I pressed my mouth over his. I inhaled his breath. He'd had coffee with almond flavoring recently. I wished I could plunge my tongue into his mouth to see if the amaretto creamer he'd obviously used still lingered there, but I didn't. I just leaned in a little more to apply a bit more pressure. He was shorter than me but not by too much. Just the right amount. Leaner, too. God, I wanted to get my hands on him and feel those hard angles and tight muscles. His fingers came to rest on my shoulder. All the blood rushed from my head to my groin, leaving me lightheaded and as hard as a railroad spike.

I cupped his cheek, the skin smoothly shaven under my fingertips.

"Or maybe dinner first?" I asked. His reply was a rustle of hot breath fanning over my just-been-kissed lips. He wanted to say yes. I saw it in the way one side of his mouth subtly moved upward. Then that touch of a smile disappeared. The relaxed man I was exchanging breaths with turned into a statue, complete with frozen face and stony gray eyes.

"You need to go. Now. Right now." He fumbled with the doorknob.

"Why? What are you so scared of? You're the one who's out, yet you act like you're terrified to go grab a bite to eat. Shouldn't it be *me* acting all freaked out?" I stroked his face. He slapped my hand away. I gawked at him as my mind tried to catch up with the sudden about-face. "Maybe I was a little pushy kissing you and all, but—"

"Just get out!" He yanked the door open. It slapped

both of us on the hip and nearly jarred loose from his grip. I took a few steps in reverse, lifted my hands in an "I'm backing away" gesture like one would when confronted by a terrified yet angry dog.

"Okay, I'm going," I said as I stepped around the door. "I'm sorry, Layton. I just… I'm sorry." My lungs emptied and collapsed, or it felt like it. His gaze darted from his hand on the knob to me. Yep. Terrified animal fit his actions and expression well. I backed out of his space, lowered my hands, and tried to think up something calming and intelligent to say.

Layton shut the door in my face. Wow. How many times had Cole and Karrie Anne closed me out of a room the same way? I'd let him down somehow, just like I'd repeatedly let down my parents. I sucked.

"I didn't mean to disappoint you too," I exhaled over the wood I was now kissing instead of a sexy man in a suit. Layton's lips were much tastier—and less splintery—than the door. Softer, too. I trailed a finger over a hinge, then walked off. Maybe he wanted a better gift…

SEVEN

Layton

The gift on my desk was a visual reminder throughout every single meeting I had right through to the weekend. I tried putting it in the drawer, but then I imagined Adler coming in and somehow knowing it was in there and that I'd accepted it. I'd considered calling him in earlier and telling him he'd left it, but that would've meant I'd have to see him again. In my office. This tiny cramped space with no windows. Adler was scheduled in for a session, but he'd already canceled twice, and part of me was happy about that. Of course, the professional side of me abhorred the fact that he wasn't receiving the right information and education, but I wasn't ready to see him again, not yet.

All because of that kiss.

From wanting more all the way through to panicking had taken no more than a few seconds, but it had felt like forever. There was a reason every lover I'd had since college had been smaller than me, or at least less of a physical presence than Adler was. I'd felt suffocated even as I was turned on, and I replayed in my head the words that my therapist had taught me in my darker days. *I'm strong. It wasn't my fault.*

The words were hollow; momentarily I had felt out of control, and I didn't like the feeling.

So I hid the gift under a folder on my desktop and tried to ignore it, pushing it and the folder right to the edge.

The team had left on a road trip that afternoon, and the only meeting I'd had before they left was with Ten, who seemed to me to be getting more nervy with each passing day. I'd noticed that Jared held his hand in meetings, and that when Ten was alone with me he fidgeted a lot. I made a mental note to sit down with him for a longer chat.

Felix Cote poked his head around the door with an accompanying knock, and I smiled up at him.

The team owner was a big bear of a man; a true seventies hockey player. There were photos of him in the corridor in all kinds of bad outfits, from seventies flares to a full-on eighties mullet. When he interviewed my firm for this position, he'd talked at length about playing against some guy called Mario, whom I didn't know from Adam, but it turned out now owned a team of his own and was considered to be a hot player. The only name I'd known before coming here was Gretzky, and that had only been because a kid on my floor at college had a motivational poster of him with wise words about chances, or scoring, or something like that.

You'd better believe I researched Mario, and Felix, and the whole seventies/eighties environment that surrounded hockey.

Right now, Felix looked very calm and collected, unlike in the original meeting where, to put it bluntly, he'd been close to losing his shit at any given moment. While everyone around him saw the Ten/Jared situation as a chance to promote equality and give the team a positive marketing spin, all he could see was the amount of money the team would lose if butts left seats. I didn't blame him; after all it was his investment on the line.

"How's it going?" he asked.

I gave formal written reports daily, although I wasn't sure his PA, Jane, passed them up to her boss. She probably summarized them for the man, who seemed to be constantly wheeling and dealing with an eye to taking the Railers to the top of the league.

"Good." I reached over for the folder of information I was compiling, along with the infant marketing plan, and gestured for him to come in. I assumed he wanted details, but it soon became apparent that he had something else on his mind.

"So, I was thinking…" He stopped, turned around, and shut the door behind him. I didn't feel panicked, not like when I'd had the team in there, which was stupid, because Felix was just as big, and fit for his age. "May I sit?" he asked, ever so politely, and I nodded.

"Of course. Is something wrong?" Worry gripped me. Was he there to say Ten and Jared had changed their minds, or that he didn't want me working on this?

He coughed to clear his throat. "My wife, bless her soul, married to me thirty years and counting, a good woman who's put up with a lot over the years what with hockey and… well, hockey is everything, really. She said I needed some sensitivity training."

If I hadn't had so much experience at schooling my expression, my eyes would have been wide and my mouth would have been hanging open. I'd never expected the owner of the team to get involved.

"Sure, we can do that."

Felix sat back in his seat. "Can you do it now?" he asked.

I had the impression he wanted to do it then because the team was away. The arena emptied for road trips, apparently, all but some admin staff and the general employees working other events.

"Of course." I pushed the marketing plan to one side and reached for the other information, at the same time knocking the temporary gift-hiding stationery onto the floor. Felix reached down and picked up the small wrapped gift.

"Is it your birthday? Did we miss it? You should tell Jane and she'll pick up a cake or something like she does for the rest of us."

"No, my birthday is November," I said.

I reached out for the offered gift, tucking it in the drawer along with all thoughts of what Adler would say if he knew where it was. Felix looked like he was going to say something else, but I headed him off at the pass.

"Tell me where you'd like to start."

He sighed and squirmed in the chair. Even though I'd swapped the smaller chair for one that actually allowed hockey asses to fit, it was still a tight fit.

"So, when I played, it was the seventies, and things were..." He searched for the right word, a thoughtful expression on his face. "Different," he offered, with a shrug to indicate how lame he thought it was. "When I played... hell, sexuality, gender, it wasn't the issue it is now."

He held up a hand to stop me, clearly expecting me to argue that those things had been an issue for the longest time. He didn't know that was the last thing I'd do. The history of equality has been a bumpy road that's still being fixed on a daily basis, but I knew to frame people's experiences based on their age, or even the state or country they were born in.

He paused again, then exhaled noisily. "I remember one day, in the early eighties, the worst chirp was using the whole AIDS thing to piss a rival off. You know, that was shit then, and it was still something guys used throughout that decade. In the seventies there was this whole Russian–US Cold War thing, but that died. Am I making any sense?"

He looked at me hopefully, like I'd be able to help just from that short explanation. Lucky for him, I could.

"Absolutely," I said, and leaned forward. Explaining how there were a hundred factors in how you spoke or what your beliefs were was a simple thing. The last thing I wanted with any of the older staff was resentment that I was telling them their actions twenty years ago had been shameful. I had to be pragmatic and explain clearly how things had changed.

When he left, he hesitated by the door, "You should come to dinner Tuesday, when the boys are back. Lillian will expect you and be happy to see you. You could meet the team in less formal surroundings."

I so did not want to be at any dinner with any of the team, but this was a suck-it-up situation, and I could hope Adler wouldn't be one of the skaters there.

"That would be lovely," I said formally.

"Jane will email you," he said, and left, leaving the door open, as I liked it.

True to his word, the email arrived at the same time as Edgar at the door. Edgar was part of the communications team, a reluctant supporter of the team Twitter account. He knocked, and I smiled at him the same way I had at Felix.

He looked gray.

I instantly thought the worst. "What happened?" I asked.

Mutely, he handed over his iPhone, and I saw Arvy's Twitter. I knew it wasn't Arvy who had posted the short sentence. I knew Arvy. He was a good guy, very respectful, and this was someone else who'd taken his phone.

The message was simple and involved a joke about women. *Great.* I went into action mode.

Within ten minutes the tweet was deleted and the culprit—one of the junior equipment guys, a kid of no more than eighteen—was relieved of his job. Not my call. That was all Felix, who blustered and cursed and talked about the Railers family and how one bad apple could ruin everything.

I knew it could, but I didn't panic, and managed the situation.

By the time I left the office, I was more exhausted than when the team was in and out of my office for their sensitivity chats.

But I didn't sleep. Because, hey, who needs sleep anyway? All I could think of was Adler and his stupid gift and the casual way he talked about his family and their complete lack of interest in him. Or at least that was what I'd got from his little speech.

Then my thoughts changed, became less concerned with work, the pen, or Adler's family. No, this was more about that kiss and the brief moment when I'd actually enjoyed being held and kissed like that.

Before the panic had set in.

***

TUESDAY CAME around way too fast. I'd managed to avoid talking to my mom for most of that, but when she pinned me down, it turned out she wanted me home for Thanksgiving.

"Just one day when I have all my babies under one roof," she'd said.

Actually she said that every year, and she deserved us all to be there, but I had work to do, and the announcement had been set for two days after Thanksgiving, which was only two weeks away. The date had been chosen to fall between two home games, and my next job was to coach Ten and Jared in what to say in answer to questions. I'd seen them both briefly that morning, and Ten had looked less shifty, like maybe getting away from Harrisburg had been a good thing for him.

Of course they'd won all three of their away games, so the entire team was on a high.

The entire team was also at this damn dinner.

Finding Felix's house was easy; his was the huge mansion at the end of a cul-de-sac. Getting in was harder, as there was a speaker you had to talk into, and it crackled a lot. In the end I followed a scarlet Ferrari in, and sighed when I saw that it was Arvy getting out. I hadn't seen him since the whole tweet incident. He saw me and stopped me before I even spoke.

"New code on my phone lock, and it never leaves my side," he said, and waved his phone at me like that proved how responsible he was being. "And I did what you said and tweeted the apology, and a picture of my dog, and another of me without a shirt."

"I saw," I said, with a twitch of a smile.

"Cool," he replied, then walked at my side up the length of the long driveway to the imposing front of the house.

"So you going home for Thanksgiving?" I asked when we ran out of conversation that wasn't about Twitter. It wasn't like I could talk hockey, although I was learning from my *Dummies* book and watching so many old recordings on YouTube that I could explain the game with some authority. I just hadn't tried it on a hockey player yet for fear of being laughed at. And it was a very long driveway. I considered laying my Mario Lemieux knowledge on him, but even that had its limits.

"Nah," he said. "We have a game either side of it, and the guys will meet up at someone's house here. You?"

"Probably not."

We reached the front door and knocked, and a woman answered who I knew was Lillian, Felix's wife. Small, immaculately dressed in a simple black dress with pearls, she welcomed us in and showed me around a little. There were so many photos of the teams that Felix had played for, from old black-and-white photos of a kid, right up to the signing ceremony for the Railers franchise.

Along with Arvy, all of the players were ranged in a large reception room, making the place look untidy. I knew it was only a matter of time before I found Adler. Luckily, that didn't happen until dinner. Unluckily, Lillian sat me right next to him, with Stan on my other side.

"Hey," he said, and moved in his chair, his thigh against mine. I moved as well, away from him, knocking my water in the process and nearly spilling it.

"Hello." I said. "So I saw you won your three games." Safe subject. Hockey information I could talk about; team wins and losses.

"Yeah," he said. "It was one of those road trips where everything gelled. A good bonding exercise. Nice to get to know the guys a bit more."

The starter was served, a mushroom soup sprinkled with parsley, along with crunchy bread, and thankfully

Felix began talking about the road trip and how pleased he was. There was wine; I stuck to water.

"Good," Stan said, nudging me in the side and nearly causing me to fall the other way into Adler's lap. I looked sideways at him and waited for more. He indicated my mushroom soup and repeated that single word. "Good."

"Yeah," I said. "Da," I added.

"Snow sicks," he added, and narrowed his eyes at me. I got the feeling I was being warned off of doing something there. I thought he'd said snow sicks, or maybe no sicks, or... who the hell knew what he'd said? "Eat."

"Okay," I said, and carried on eating, listening to the quiet rumble of Stan's voice as he talked in low Russian to the only other guy on the team who knew what he was really saying, Anatoly Sokolov.

"He says you need to eat all your soup," Anatoly said helpfully. His voice was less growly Russian, and more American but with an accent. I knew he'd been playing for US teams for the last ten years, so there was hope that one day Stan would become more understandable, or more likely that the team would learn enough Russian.

"I am," I said, and pointedly scooped up another spoonful of soup and swallowed it. I even exaggerated the action, and felt like I was receiving approval from both Russians.

"He says you must eat and not make yourself sick," Anatoly added.

I glanced at Stan. What? He just smiled at me, but not in a friendly, open way—more in an understanding, sympathetic way. What the hell?

"He says he sees chocolate on your desk a lot, and coffee. Too much coffee."

I felt like everyone was looking at me, but a quick glance showed me that no one was paying any attention.

"Okay," I said to Stan and Anatoly.

They both nodded at me, but in my peripheral vision, I caught Stan looking at me. I ignored him, trying to focus on something else. I zeroed in on one particular conversation, then wished I hadn't.

"So I said, sixty-nine plus me is the number seventy I wear on my back." Denton was talking. He was a winger, and sitting the other side of Adler. I liked Denton, but he was a bit of an idiot, who made jokes about everything.

"She fell for your shit?" Arvy asked.

Evidently I'd tripped into listening to Denton explaining a pickup line.

"Yeah, she was hot to trot, and the sixty-nine..." He trailed off and looked at me past Adler. "My bad," he said. But he was smiling like he wasn't apologizing at all. And hell, why was he even apologizing to me? My mouth opened before my brain kicked in, the very thing I'd warned the entire team about. And what I said fell into an unfortunate lull in conversation.

"Hell, what is it with hockey players and their addiction to sixty-nine?"

Silence.

Complete, stone-cold silence.

And then the laughter started, and right in the middle of it I could feel myself turning scarlet. This was like I was back at college; this was me saying something idiotic and having people turn on me. I was hot, and I pushed back my chair, aiming for composed.

"Excuse me," I said.

And before anyone could stop me, before I'd finished the soup that Stan so desperately wanted me to; I left.

EIGHT

Adler
___

I watched Layton bolt from the table. Well, maybe bolt wasn't the right word. He didn't leap up or knock over his chair. Nothing that dramatic. But he did hustle his ass away from the meal and the confused Railers. Everyone sat looking at each other, but no one offered to get up. Probably I should have just continued eating the gourmet food in front of me, but no. Adler Lockhart was just not capable of such intelligence.

Without saying a word, I dabbed at my mouth with the cloth napkin, pushed to my feet, and ambled off in Layton's wake. The guys began to murmur among themselves. I exited through the heavy front door and instantly saw Layton standing among all the parked cars, looking lost.

I walked over to him, my mind coughing up stupid things to say. The closer I got to him, the thicker his cloud of anxiety grew. Arousal was the cloud clinging to me. His steely gaze flew to me when I rounded the bumper of a massive black SUV. The man looked close to losing his shit.

"Someone blocked me in," he panted, and tugged on

his neatly knotted tie. I gave the SUV a look, then glanced back at Layton.

"I can take you home."

Okay, Adler. What the ever-loving fuck?

"No, no, I can't do that. Uh, do you know who that behemoth belongs to?" He indicated the Ford Explorer with a nod of his head.

"Not a clue." His nerves were contagious. I started fiddling with the tie resting a bit too tightly on my Adam's apple as well. "I'm parked in the street." I motioned to my BMW parked a few houses down. "I do that so it won't get dinged. Did you even open my gift?"

Okay, Adler. What the ever-loving fuck part deux.

"The gift? No, I didn't open it," he said.

"Yeah, I figured. It's okay. I shouldn't have asked." I took a step closer. His rat-trapped-in-a-room-full-of-cats vibe was off the charts. "Look, what you said in there," I jerked a thumb at the expensive home filled with puck pushers, "was just a joke. A funny one too, you know."

He didn't return my smile. He began wetting his lips, moving in a tight circle like an antique tin top that I'd had as a kid. It was all kinds of sexy. Well, the tin top wasn't sexy. He was. His lips were slick and shiny now. They needed to be kissed again. Yep. By me. Right there in the driveway against the SUV that was freaking him out. Sexy toys. I bet he'd be an amazing man to play adult games with…

Adler, stop thinking about sexy toys. Please. You're starting to sound like an idiot.

"I let my mouth take over for my brain. That's not acceptable. Why did this prick park here?" He slapped at the SUV. I winced in expectation of an alarm going off, but the massive thing sat there quietly.

"Because it's a driveway," I pointed out. "Do you like

coffee? I mean, I know you drink coffee, because when I kissed you I could smell amaretto creamer on your breath, and unless you chug creamer straight then you must put it in coffee. So you want to go have some coffee? I'm parked over there." Again, I waved a hand at my car sitting by the curb.

Layton stared at me, his cheeks still flushed and his eyes... oh man, those gray eyes were brimming with emotion. Not sure that they were good feelings, but his eyes were gorgeous, and I found myself suddenly not caring whether he opened my gift. I'd buy him another one. A better one. One that would make him see how much I liked him.

"No, Adler, no coffee. I just..." He stopped pacing like a nervous lion and exhaled dramatically, his chest expanding and stretching the snappy jacket hugging his lean frame and making me a tiny bit hungrier for the taste and feel of him. "We can't date, Adler."

"Why not?" I shoved my hands into the front pockets of my pants.

"Because... because of a lot of reasons."

I ran my fingers over the couple of coins in my pocket. "What reasons? I'm not a serial killer. I don't smoke or do drugs. I only have a beer now and again. I'm funny and reasonably cute in a Fred Weasley kind of way. I don't play for Pittsburgh or Philly. I'd like to buy you coffee and talk about shit. Get to know you. Maybe kiss you again. We can call it something else if the word 'date' worries you. How about a coffee klatch? Like we're a couple of old women sitting down to gossip over coffee. Will you do a klatch with me?"

There seemed to be something on the tip of his tongue. His wild eyes settled a bit as he tried to look at me without it being obvious that he was staring at me.

It reminded me of that time Apollo and I had found a stunned bird lying in a flower bed. It had flown into one of the windows of the Lockhart Maine summer home. We'd sat down in the mulch and taken turns holding that chickadee until it opened its eyes. It had sat in my hands for a moment, dark eyes trying to assess where it was and what kind of predator was looking at it. In a flurry of fear and an overwhelming need to be free, I assumed, it had taken wing.

Layton reminded me of that fearful bird.

He dug into the interior pocket of his jacket and pulled out his phone. "Thank you for the klatch offer, but I'm not sure it would be wise professionally. I'm calling a cab."

"But I have a car forty feet away," I told him, and pointed at the Beemer yet again. "Dude, come on, let me—"

"I can't. I just… No. I can't."

"Right, okay, it's cool. Don't pay for a cab. Just hang here and let me go find out who's blocking you. Okay?"

He nodded and lowered his phone from his ear. "Thank you."

Five minutes later, Layton was pulling out in his Nissan Leaf, which was way too quiet for comfort as I stood next to Denton, the owner of the SUV.

"I don't know anyone else who drives those electric cars," Denton said.

"Me neither."

Denton cleared his throat. "Did he leave because of that joke? Was it offensive to gays?"

"Nah, man, he left because of me." I sauntered to my car parked beside the curb and deserted the dinner as well. My partying mood had left at the same time Layton did.

"ARE you sure you don't want any more pie?" Apollo lingered by the fridge, pie in hand, eager to finish cleaning up after the meal.

"Nope. If I eat one more bite, I'll die." I pushed myself up from the dining room table, which we hardly ever used aside from holiday meals, and patted my protruding stomach. "I plan to go take a nap in front of the Vikings–Lions game."

"You should call Karrie Anne," Apollo said while shoving the dessert into the fridge. He had to wiggle the remains of the Thanksgiving turkey, bowls of corn, stuffing, mashed potatoes, and cranberry sauce around.

"Maybe Karrie Anne should call *me*," I mumbled as I waddled from the dining room to the living room.

"Maybe she should, but she probably won't," Apollo called after me.

"Yeah, I know." I dove onto the sofa, the huge sectional swallowing me up. I felt like absolute shit now. Layton had neatly avoided me since that dinner at the owner's house. I kept canceling our meetings because I knew he was uncomfortable around me but didn't know why. Rolling onto my back, I fished my phone out of the front pocket of my jeans, unbuttoned the top of my pants, and lay there staring at my smartphone. No calls. No texts. Wow. Holidays were so much fun. I was really feeling the Norman Rockwell. Not.

"Call her," Apollo called from the kitchen. "Maybe she'll surprise you." I could hear that even *he* didn't believe the words coming out of his mouth. Probably his mom had told him to nudge me into calling. Moms are like that. Warm and caring. Or so I've heard.

"Maybe my dick will be gilded the next time I look too," I shouted, and got a snort in reply.

I hit Karrie Anne's contact picture and put the phone

against my ear. Feet on the arm of the couch, I waited and waited. Finally she picked up. I could hear laughter and chit-chat behind her. Oh right, the yearly Thanksgiving meal in Punta Cana with Dad's clients and Mom's golf club sisters.

"Adler, how are you, sweetheart?" She sounded like she actually cared. I wondered how much she'd had to drink. "Your father was just talking about you. Why aren't you here?"

"I have this thing called a career." I didn't ask why Cole was talking about me or what he'd been saying. None of it was good, I was sure. Probably he was shitfaced and lamenting what a disappointment his only child was. Queer jocks weren't high on his "Things I Love" list.

"Oh yes, hockey. Well, are you winning your games?" She whispered to someone to shush, then giggled in my ear.

"Yeah, we're doing pretty good actually. I mean, for a new expansion team we're coming together well. The guys on my line are pretty decent and…"

She'd started chatting with someone named Adolphus. I waited. She continued to talk to this Adolphus, giggling and whispering naughty little things.

"You do recall that your son is listening to all this, right?" I asked after several minutes of her trying to flirt with Adolphus.

"Adler? When did you call? My God, I must have had more Manhattans than I realized. I have to go now. Ta."

She hung up. I flung the phone onto the table, closed my eyes, and wondered how normal families did holidays.

"Okay, the cleaning up is over. Time to start decorating!" Apollo shouted, then rang jingly sleigh bells right in my face. I squeezed my eyes tightly shut.

Ho ho fucking ho.

TODAY WAS THE DAY. The day the Railers management and team stood behind two of our own as they came out to the world. One day after Black Friday. One day before our first game of the season with Boston. Both were big deals for vastly different reasons. One day was for big sales and the other day would be for big hits. Yeah, I thought that up all by myself as I shaved and dressed for the press event. I'd gotten the official email from Layton Foxx. At first, my heart had sped up seeing his name, but then as I read it I'd realized it was purely a business discussion. How he wanted us to act, dress, and several politically correct replies for after the press were done feasting on Tennant and Jared.

I'd linger in the shadows and watch. Maybe I could get a feel for how the world would take gay hockey players before I leaped off the cliff. Everyone was always telling me to shut up and think, so that was what I was doing. Was hiding the same as thinking? Somehow it didn't feel like it.

As I drove to the barn, thoughts of Layton swirled around inside my head. That was nothing new. The man was starting to be an obsession. He prowled my dreams. I'd woken up several times over the past week or two soaked in sweat, my cock hot and hard, with flimsy remnants of sleepy visions of Layton clinging to my consciousness. The man was always naked in my dreams. Eager, too. Pliant and supple under my hands, willing… ah man, so willing. And every time I woke up in that state, I jerked off to the tattered fragments of erotica. I hadn't beaten off this much since I was fifteen. My fucking dick was going to be calloused if I kept this up.

Sitting at a red light, Winger on the stereo, I mulled over how the three most important players in this press event had to be feeling. Tennant and Jared were probably hot, nervous messes. Layton too, I'd wager. He was high-strung anyway. I glanced to the right and saw a small boutique. Classy, by the looks. Maybe I should grab them all a little something. I checked my Rolex. Plenty of time. Flipping the turn signal on, I slid out of traffic and parked.

The inside of the tiny shop was nice. It was a high-end gift shop with some jewelry. Hand-crafted, according to the filigreed signs. Inside the glass were some quality men's gifts. I settled on cuff links for Rowe and Madsen. Matching silver ones—square, classic and simple. They fit the men, or so I felt. Layton would be trickier. None of the jewelry felt like him. I meandered around, checking things out: pretty trinkets and little wooden boxes for earrings or bangles. Silken scarves, frilly shawls, brightly colored ties. Then I found a box holding a silk handkerchief. It was eggshell white with a vibrant rainbow thread hand-stitched around the scalloped edges. Folded and tucked into the pocket of one of his tailored suits, it would the perfect accessory for a hot, professional gay man.

Ten minutes later I was back in my car, Winger's "Can't Get Enuff" vibrating out of the speakers, my gifts lying on the passenger seat.

"Jesus," I murmured when I slid into the players' entrance. You could hear the hum of the press gathered in the large room set aside for the media. I slipped past the open door, avoiding the reporters, and hurried into the dressing room. The Railers had turned out *en masse* to give Ten and Jared support. Sure, there had been gentle pokes from Layton as well as the other people in PR and social media to attend, but no one had been forced. As I scanned the room for Rowe and Madsen, I counted the whole team and coaching staff.

I strolled up to Arvy and Stan. I got a grin from one

and a clap on the back from the other. Stan stood at my side with his hand lingering on my shoulder.

"You guys seen Ten or Coach Madsen?" I enquired.

"They're off with that Foxx guy getting tips or something. You got them gifts? Shit." Arvy sighed. "I didn't get them anything. Now I feel like foot fungus."

"You are no foot fungus. You are spray to kill fungus," Stan announced loudly enough to quiet those standing around us.

"Yep, that's him, Arvy Funky Toes," I tossed out. Stan laughed loud and long. Arvy punched me in the arm.

After a short visit with more of my fellow Railers, I went off to find the stars of this gay little production. All three were gathered in Layton's claustrophobic office. They all looked up when I rapped on the open door.

"Hey, Lockhart," Madsen said.

My gaze locked onto Layton. He was in a black suit with a white shirt and a slim silver tie that made his pewter eyes glow. There was a softness in his gaze when it met mine. My stomach did a wicked backward flip.

"Did you need something?" Madsen added.

"Uh, no. I just wanted to give you all a good luck gift." I rammed a box at each man one by one, Layton getting the final present. His eyebrows knotted up as Tennant and Jared tore into their gifts. "Mom always says nothing says love like a small box with a big chunk of gold inside it."

Ten and Jared chortled at my *bon mot*. Layton merely stood there, box in one hand and iPad in the other, trying to stare holes through me.

"Whoa, Ad, man, these are nice," Tennant said as he inspected his cuff links.

"They truly are. Thanks, Adler, but you didn't have to go to all this trouble. Seeing you and the rest of the Railers here backing Ten and me is a wonderful gift."

I shook Jared's hand, then Ten's.

"Let's go grab ten minutes alone somewhere. I need to replace my cuff links," Ten told his boyfriend, then gave me a solid rap side of fist to side of fist.

"Is that what they're calling it now?" I asked with a dirty chuckle. Ten pounded me on the shoulder, then left with Madsen on his heels.

"You going to open that one?" I asked Layton when it was just him, me, and that box in his hand.

"Adler, you have to stop buying me gifts. It's unprofessional and it makes me feel beholden and I don't much care to feel that way." He held the box out to me. I shook my head. He frowned and lowered the prettily wrapped box. "This isn't the way to win my heart."

"Then what *is* the way to win your heart?"

He blew out a slow breath through pursed lips. "I could use a cup of coffee."

It was ridiculous how excited hearing him say that made me. "Like a coffee date?"

"Well, it won't be much of a date, since there's a whole hockey team and about a hundred members of the press corps here. Maybe just a coffee klatch this time?"

"Cool. Klatches are cool. Will you open that gift sometime?" I tapped the box in his left hand with my finger. He nodded. Then I ran my finger up his thumb and over his knuckles. He didn't jerk his hand away, so yay for progress.

"I have to get to the press conference," he reminded me as I traced the tendons on the back of his hand. It would have been the most natural thing in the world to kiss him then. But I couldn't, because I was still hiding my gay man in a dark, dank closet.

"I'm buying," I stated, then drew back before I threw aside caution just to feel his lips against mine again.

"No, I am." He placed gift number two on his desk, then slipped around me.

We argued all the way to the coffee machine outside the physical therapy room. In the end, I let him buy because it made him happy. Making him happy made me freaking radiant.

"Can men be radiant, or is that a term best saved for pregnant women and Disney princesses?" I asked him.

His unamused look said it all. "Stop canceling our meetings."

I suspected my days of skipping out on us alone in any room were over.

NINE

Layton

I knew why I'd said coffee would be good, whether it was the klatch type or could be considered a date. It was the only thing I could think of to get Adler out of my office. Not because I felt claustrophobic with him in there, though; I'd actually got used to the way he filled the room now. It was more how when he touched me I felt like I was losing control, and I was damn sure I couldn't lose control around Adler anytime soon.

The coffee was shit, but at least it gave my mouth something to do, even though my stomach was still a mess of knots as each minute toward the presser slipped past.

"You okay?" Adler asked, concern showing in the small frown between his eyes.

I shook my head, then checked my watch. Thirty minutes, and there was already the buzz of talking in the press room. I knew that because I'd peeked around the door like a five-year-old at his first Nativity looking for his parents a little earlier. I'd hand-selected some of the journalists, ones I trusted to be supportive, and they were all there except Bryan from OutSportsPA, who promised he'd make it. I was relying on Bryan to be the one to ask the intelligent questions after the big announcement. Pulling the press room door shut, I'd sent out a small prayer that Bryan was heading in soon.

"I'm fine," I lied, and sipped at the coffee, wincing as the burned beans taste flowed over my tongue. The last thing I needed was coffee; I was hyper. Maybe Stan had a point about my coffee consumption.

He touched me again; he did that a lot. Casual touches that were more about attraction than reassurance. I could see the heat in his eyes, I could recall the feel of his lips on mine, and I wanted him so bad.

"It will go great," he reassured me, and I'd opened my mouth to tell him I wasn't worried when I heard the shouting. At first it was just a mess of noise, and then I heard specific words; ugly sounds that had me dropping my coffee in the trash and sprinting down the corridor, landing right in the middle of a face-off.

Ten had his hand on Jared's arm. Jared was standing stoic and silent. An older man was shouting at him; I didn't know who the hell it was. Then I saw a younger man. I knew that was Jared's son, Ryker Everett, who'd said he wanted to be with his dad for this announcement. I liked the kid, but he was just as angry as the old man, and I couldn't get my head around what was happening.

I barreled right into the middle of the group, even as the old guy was swinging a fist with intent to hurt. I ducked and felt the movement of air when the fist passed through where I'd been standing. The old man stepped back, off-balance, but he was still spouting hate.

"What do you think will happen to Ryker now? The son of a fucking fag. He'll be dead in the water. You've fucked his draft chances—"

"Enough," I said.

"Grandad, stop it," Ryker said at the same time, grabbing the old man's fist, which had moved dangerously close again. My brain put everything together. This was Jimmy Everett, former NHL star, Jared's sort of ex-father-in-law. I know Jared and his girlfriend, Everett's daughter, didn't marry, but I wasn't sure how else to label Everett. He was an old school hockey player who I'd been told had already caused one scene on the property.

"Someone call security," I snapped, and pressed a hand to Jimmy's chest. "Sir, you need to leave."

Jimmy snarled, his whole demeanor one of hate, and for a second or two I felt utter fear, then somehow, with Jared trying to pull me away and Adler right there at my side, fear left me in an instant.

"I want Dad to come out," Ryker said loudly. Loudly enough to be heard over his posturing grandfather, but also likely enough to be heard in reception. I wanted to tell him to quieten it down a bit, but hell, Jared was staring at his son, and this seemed like a family moment.

"You don't know what this will mean—"

"Yes, Grandad, I do. It will give every other player the chance to love who they want to love, and to play the game, and not to be judged."

Ryker was working up a full head of steam now, but his voice broke at the end, and Jared stepped forward to place a hand on his son's arm.

"Ryker," he began.

"No, Dad," Ryker said. "Don't reassure me, or tell me that maybe Grandad has a point in any of this. I'm fucked off with hearing it all."

"I wasn't going to—"

But Ryker wasn't listening. He rounded on his grandad and poked him in the chest. Hard. "What if I fell for a guy, huh, Grandad? Would you be so willing to push me into being your golden boy if I turned out to be bi?"

"Ryker, for God's sake, keep your voice down," Jimmy said. "This is how rumors get started."

Ryker's face was like stone, and he crossed his arms over his chest. "I kissed a boy at Christmas, and he's coming to my eighteenth birthday party next week."

Jimmy went pale. Jared's eyes widened. Ten's mouth fell open. And me? I was in the middle of some great family reveal that was getting out of hand and needed to be corralled somewhere private. Not so that people didn't hear, but just so the family could talk in peace.

And then the shit really hit the fan. Some great temper erupted from Jimmy, and he yanked Ryker closer until they were inches apart, snarling something at him.

"What happening?" a thick Russian voice asked from the corridor we'd run down. One I recognized—Stan. "Drop Jared's boy," he ordered. Jimmy released his hold on Ryker, looked right at Stan, and paled, taking a step back. But it didn't seem to stop him.

"Selfish, fucking selfish Jared, not a single thought for me, for how you're ruining my life. And look what you've done to Ryker!"

Everyone froze when Ryker yanked him back and turned him so they were face to face.

"Dad and I have talked about this. You really think I want him to live a lie just so I don't have to face adversity in my career? And now I've told you about me, but you think it matters to me who he fell in love with?" He had both hands on Jimmy's arm and was shaking him. I stepped closer, within reach; I had to manage this, needed to be the one in control.

"Ryker—"

"No, Grandpa, you don't get to do this today. I don't

want to see you; I don't want to hear from you. We're done."

"Ryker," Jared said from behind me, his voice broken. Fuck. I'd walked into a freaking nightmare. "Think about this."

Ryker grimaced. "Oh Dad, believe me, I have. I can't love someone who hates like he does." He stepped back from his grandpa, releasing his hold, and the old man slumped a little. For a second I had visions of him having a heart attack, or falling to his knees, or crying, but no, he pulled his shoulders back and squared off to Jared, Ten, and his grandson.

"Then I'm done with you. And you," he pointed at his grandson, "consider the check for your eighteenth birthday torn to pieces, and you think about this when all you get is beer league on the weekends."

"Who even uses checks anymore?" Ryker snapped.

Jimmy full-on growled, then stalked away, thankfully in the opposite direction to the press room. But, what if he talked? What if he put out a press release, and… My head hurt, and I went into crisis mode. Something I'd seen pricked at me, and inspired, I turned to Stan.

"Tell him not to say a word until after the presser," I said.

Stan nodded and bypassed us, muttering something in Russian.

"Don't hurt him," I added instantly.

Stan stopped and turned, looking affronted. "I won't hurt," he said. "Just warn."

Jared, Ten and Ryker were in a tight hug, and Adler was close to me; so close I could feel the heat of him, and briefly I leaned in to his strength, just needing that moment of connection.

"Adler," I said. I didn't know what I was asking, but somehow Adler knew.

"I'll go with Stan and witness the warning," he murmured. Then, with a squeeze of my arm, he followed Stan.

How had he known I needed that? This seemingly self-absorbed hockey player intent on getting me into bed who refused to take no for an answer?

I turned to Jared and Ten, and they'd separated from their hug and were now looking at me expectantly.

Oh yeah, I needed to have all the answers now. I watched as Jared put an arm around his son, and examined the open affection between them. It reminded me of a time when I used to welcome that sort of affection from my family, but hell, I wasn't going to focus on that right now.

I adjusted my tie and brushed imaginary dirt from my suit jacket, straightening it.

A quick glance at my watch had the time at twenty minutes to go, and I wondered how something so dramatic had taken up only ten minutes of time when it had felt like a lifetime.

I didn't have time to go after Jimmy, or to check on the limits of Stan's intimidation; I had to trust Adler. I had to make sure that everyone was calm, and reassure them all.

"Hey, little brother," a deep voice came from my left. *What now?*

I heard Ten yelp, and turned to see a guy sweep him up in a hug that seemed endless. This was Brady Rowe, the eldest of Ten's brothers, who played for Boston, if memory served me right. I knew it was either Boston or Florida, the other team with a Rowe brother. I knew that because I'd reached out to both teams in all of this; after all, they'd be affected as well, given the connection to Tennant Rowe.

The hockey world was this mess of interconnections and gossip that I needed to cut off at the knees. Boston had actually suggested I work with them after I'd finished with the Railers. That was the work I liked to get, and I had most of the protocols pretty solid in my head.

I just needed to work out how everything needed to be tweaked after this presser.

"Jamie wanted to come."

"I know he's playing on the West Coast tonight," Ten said, and hugged his brother again.

I can't remember the last time I hugged one of my brothers. Not since the night Zach carried me indoors and cried with me. Not since my siblings stopped being able to look me in the eyes.

When everyone separated, Stan and Adler were back.

"We put him in a closet," Adler said in all seriousness. "The irony," he added.

"You didn't," I began, and then Adler elbowed Stan in the side.

"Of course we didn't. Stan just stood there and glared, and I suggested he hold off on commenting until after the press conference." He smiled at me. "So it's up to you to make sure this presser is enough to stop the critics."

No pressure, then.

I felt even sicker than earlier.

Jared, Ten, Ryker and Brady moved away toward the press room, Stan ambling after them, still muttering in Russian, God knew what about.

I just stared at Adler, probably looking like a lobster being held over a pot of water. He was still smiling, and gripped my arm, squeezing a little.

"Breathe," he said.

So I did.

· · ·

THE ROOM WASN'T PARTICULARLY large, but was big enough for thirty or so chairs with some attending journalists standing at the back. I spotted Bryan immediately, and we exchanged nods. I hadn't told him everything, but he only had to look at the names on the podium to have a good idea of what was happening here.

Jared Madsen. Tennant Rowe.

Most of the team were there, ranged down the sides of the room. The leadership group, the captain, both of the alternates, the veterans, Jared's son and Ten's oldest brother were in a loose group right by the small stage. Brady was in a Boston sweatshirt, out of place among the team guys in their suits. But he was a statement that needed to be made; that it wasn't just the Railers who were facing this today. Brady was both family and a representative of an original six team.

And yes, I'd looked up what that meant when Ten had explained that his brother was up his own ass about being in a team with history. I'd thought it might be an issue, and said so, but Ten and Jared had just laughed. Clearly big-brother-Boston-player wasn't an issue.

Between the two groups stood Adler.

Seemed to me that everyone was there to support Ten and Jared, except for Adler, who was there for me. I shook my head to rid myself of the idiot thought, but Adler wasn't looking at the stage; he was staring right at me.

The owner of the team, Felix Cote, stood up. "Welcome, everyone," he said, settling the room as Ten and Jared took their seats. "We have a prepared statement, and there will be copies available at the door. Tennant and Jared will take limited questions afterward."

I waited as Felix took a seat. We'd talked this through, who should read the statement. Jared had said it should be him, but I'd made my point and they'd listened.

It didn't matter who spoke the words. Jared could be perceived as leading Ten astray, or being a bad influence. Ten could talk and make it sound like Jared had changed him somehow, like maybe he was a kid who didn't know his own mind.

In the end we'd compromised.

Only when Ten started to talk did I relax a little. We'd rehearsed this. I'd warned them to stay on script. They could do this.

"I'm gay," Ten said simply. This wasn't the results of a talent show that needed long pauses—this was direct and to the point. "I've known this for a long time, although I've only recently felt the need to tell everyone about the person I truly am and about the man I'm in a committed relationship with."

"That would be me," Jared said. "I'm friends with the Rowe family, having played with Brady. When Ten was traded here from Dallas, we reconnected as friends, and then fell in love."

I nodded. The distinction had to be drawn that they'd been friends first, and that this wasn't a hangover from some teenage thing. We'd decided no one needed to know about the early kiss the two had shared.

Now it was Ten's turn again. "When I was younger I always aspired to be like my brothers. Brady and Jamie were both drafted to NHL teams, and when we practiced as kids, I was just as quick as they were, I could shoot like they could. I was a crap defenseman, and my goalie skills were for shit, but I was a good shooter. I wasn't any different from my brothers; I was just a skater."

A few of the journalists turned their heads to look at Brady, who smiled at Ten.

"I didn't have brothers," Jared said, "and I wasn't a

superstar like Ten is, but I played damn well until I had to retire on medical grounds."

I nodded again; I'd suggested they remind the audience why Jared had to stop playing. They all knew, but the fact that Jared had mentioned it meant that it would be part of their reports and posts.

"Gay wasn't the issue."

"Or bi," Jared added.

"We're still hockey players, and work hard at being the best we can."

"We can play," Jared said, "so we played."

They looked at each other then, and that wasn't scripted at all. The smile between them was beautiful, heartfelt, and I saw the flashes as people caught the images for their reports. This was the image I wanted.

Happy. Settled. In love.

"Bryan from OutSportsPA," Bryan introduced himself, "This is a question for Ten. Do you feel that now you can be true to yourself, you'll play better hockey?"

"Absolutely," Ten said, emphatic and with a smile.

"Stanley Cup better," Jared said, and nudged Ten in the side.

Ten threw him another smile, then wrapped up the interview with the thank yous. "We want to thank the Railers organization for their support in this, and for being the first professional hockey team to have to face the inevitable issues that will arise," Ten said. "I could not wish for a better team to be part of. From the owner down to the players, every single member of the team has shown compassion and understanding."

Ten's hand moved from the desk and dropped into his lap, and I just knew that he was touching Jared's knee. When Jared followed suit and then brought their joined hands up to the desk, there were more photos. We'd decided against overt PDAs just yet; our plan was to roll them out when people were more comfortable, even though I'd agreed with Jared that pulling Ten into his arms and kissing him soundly would make one hell of a statement.

Part of me hated that he couldn't do that. Well, not yet, anyway. Slow and steady wins the race.

The hand-holding was nice. A positive image that would unfortunately be enough for the haters to start the expected backlash. But also enough to show just how much these two men were in love.

I'd missed some of what Jared had said, but whatever it was had the journalists chuckling. It must have been off script, because I hadn't written anything funny in the give-and-go speech we had happening here.

And then it was done, the speech finished, and I couldn't help myself. I looked at Adler, part of me desperate for his approval of what had happened here today.

I couldn't see him, and shock that he'd left curled inside me, until I felt the touch of a hand at the small of my back.

"You did good," Adler whispered.

I relaxed a little and heard Adler's low chuckle. Bastard knew he'd got to me.

"So," Ten said, and I snapped back to the podium. "Any questions?"

"What do your brothers think?" someone asked. We'd prepped for this, but it was supposed to be Ten answering, not Brady. Only Brady being there was an added bonus.

Brady cleared his throat. "Both of his brothers are very happy not only that Ten is following his heart and is the bravest, and now happiest, person we know, but also that he's the third best player in the NHL."

The journalists laughed and some took photos of

Brady with his hands at his sides, his Boston logo front and center.

As soon as the chuckling died down, someone jumped in with another question.

"There are no protocols for an out player in the NHL. Ten, how do you think the league will react?" asked the writer for SportsWide, a pushy young guy who always got way too close to the players in post-game interviews. I'd identified him as an issue, and I could see Ten's expression changing subtly.

"I hope the league will stand by their push for inclusivity and will support our honesty," Ten said.

Clearly that wasn't enough.

"How will they stop fans wanting you off the team?" Idiot Writer persisted.

"They can try," Felix muttered under his breath. The journalists closest to the owner of the team all looked at him pointedly. He stood up, right there and then, and gave an impromptu speech that had me going hot with worry. "I have spoken to the league, to the owners of the teams in both conferences; this is an issue that will have the entire league's full support."

"So you're saying it *is* an issue?" the moron asked.

Where was Stan when you needed him to carry someone out of a room?

Felix wasn't cowed. He looked at the journalist pointedly. "As far as the league is concerned, a person's sexual preference is a non-issue."

Well, that shut him down. Of course it was an issue —no one in their right mind would assume every fan would embrace this change, or would willingly support a team that had a gay player. Not one person here was naive, but those simple words were enough to change the mood in the room from possibly confrontational if they followed the thought process of that reporter, to supportive.

The questions flew, and with every answer the mood lightened even more. This was a happy occasion, positive, and Ten and Jared, when they left, were both smiling hard.

And through it all, Adler had his hand on my back, and I reveled in the heat of him.

I was on a high—the presser had gone well, the sound-bites would be amazing, the photos good, and I knew I would be fielding requests for interviews with Jared and Ten now.

My role was far from over, but I could relax slightly.

So that was why I moved back a step until I was closer to Adler, and how, after the room emptied and it was just me and him still there, I knew what I really wanted. Post interviews could wait.

I wanted Adler. Right the hell now.

TEN

Adler

I turned to look at Layton, thinking that maybe I'd toss out something glib about more coffee and see if he'd actually-maybe-possibly go with me for a real coffee. Hell, maybe I could sweet-talk him into saying it was a date. He'd been receptive to my touches during the presser. If I was lucky, I might be able to sneak in another kiss. Talk about something my taste buds would enjoy. I bet he tasted fantastic. A sexy combination of man and coffee beans…

He leaned in a bit, his chest lightly brushing mine. My breath hitched as his cologne and the feel of his lean, hard body mingled. His gaze darted from my mouth to the two doors leading out of the press room. My focus was wholly on Layton, because holy shit he was sending out vibes that my cock was receiving loud and clear.

He wet his lips, a nervous habit that turned me right on. A group of loud males walked past the door to our left. A bit of the fire in those pewter depths disappeared.

"Can I talk to you in my office?"

"Yeah, sure."

I followed him, trying to figure out what I'd done wrong. It must have been something. Why else would he want to see me alone? Shit. Had my mouth engaged without me knowing it? We rounded a corner, my longer legs pushing to keep up with Layton's hurried pace. Dammit. I must have really hosed something up. That look I thought was desire must have been anger.

"Lockhart, you knuckle-dragging hoser," Brady Rowe shouted when he spied us coming. He'd been talking with a small group of Railers. Layton skidded to a stop in front of me. I walked up to stand at his side. He was unreadable now.

"Rowe." I slapped my hand into Brady's. He was a big guy, like me, and one hell of a defenseman. "How go things in Bean Town?"

"I can't complain. I was shocked to read you'd been traded." He gave Layton a polite nod of the head.

"Such is life in the salary cap era. It's their loss. I'm enjoying things here. You meet Layton Foxx yet? He's the Railers social media troubleshooting guru. He was the one that set this whole press thing up."

I peeked at Layton as I spoke to Brady. He looked uncertain trapped between two hulking hockey players. Not the first time I'd seen his discomfort. Why was the man so skittish? It worried me to see reserve on his handsome face. I wanted to see him only smiling. I'd work on that.

"Ten speaks highly of you, Layton." Brady shoved his big mitt at Layton, who grabbed it and gave it a quick shake, then released it. Yeah, the man was really looking hemmed in. That concerned me for reasons I didn't dare to explore right now.

"I noticed that you and Baby Brother are starting to

click on ice." Brady folded his arms over that big old Boston emblem he so proudly wore.

"Ten is an amazing center. Great eyes and soft hands. Reads a play five seconds before the other losers on the ice do."

"Which means you're always scrambling to catch up," he teased.

"Not unlike you. Defensemen are known to be a little slow, you know, up here." I tapped my temple.

"Speaking of slow, did you see that shit blowing up about Greg Davies down in the ECHL?"

"Dude, that man has issues. When he played in Columbus with me for that year, he was always wheeling chicks that I thought looked way too young to be—"

"Wait," Layton slid into the hockey talk. "This man ran over a woman with a wheel?"

Brady and I laughed. "Nah, wheeling means trying to pick up chicks," Brady explained.

"Hockey has a language all its own," Layton said, then pulled out his iPad to type something into it.

"Yeah, it does. So, look, I have a couple of hours before I have to head back to Boston. Want to meet up with me, Ten and Jared for some lunch? I guess a lot of the Railers are going too."

Hooking up with the guys and Brady sounded good. Much better than getting chewed out for some stupid social media gaffe I hadn't even been aware of making. But Layton looked set.

"Give me thirty minutes."

"Cool. We'll be hanging around talking to the press and shit. Layton, nice to meet you." Brady smiled, then went off to do his "I'm a Proud Brother of a Gay Man" thing.

Layton took off at a clip that I had to jog to match. He blew into his little office. I stepped in after him feeling like a dog about to get whipped for stealing a pork chop from a plate left on the floor. I mean, whatever I'd said, he should know better than to give me access to a pork chop. I was making no sense now. How had I got from Layton to pig meat? I needed to reel my rambling thoughts back in.

"You okay with me closing the door?" I asked.

He nodded.

I gave it a soft nudge, and it slowly drifted shut. "Okay, so here's the thing," I opened, "whatever it is that I did or said, I will apologize for it. Just write up some Tweets or something and I'll send them right out."

He made a lap around his desk, his eyes flickering from me to the door. "Lock that."

"Huh?"

"Lock the door." He stood behind his desk, smoky eyes afire. Christ. I must have really screwed the pooch. Damn pork chops.

Adler, dude, enough with the dogs and chops already.

I did as he'd asked. He walked around his desk, his gaze locked with mine, came right at me, grabbed my head with both hands, and pulled my mouth to his. The instant my lips settled on his, something shifted. The Earth's tectonic plates slid dangerously. The planet listed to the left, then came back. Layton tongued the seam of my mouth, his fingers firm on my skull. Right then I knew that whatever was happening at the core of the Earth would engulf us both. I grabbed him and slung him against the door, ravenous for more of him.

He grunted at the impact. The huff of moist breath over my face only fanned the fire. I slapped my hands against the door, his dark head resting on the wood as my fingers spread and I leaned in to him. My gaze was with his. A flare of something that had nothing to do with magma, earthquakes or lust overtook the passion in his gaze.

He was scared. Of me. Of being cornered or crowded. Okay, right. That was why he'd looked like a rabbit cornered by a couple of hounds when Brady and I had had him boxed in.

I shifted myself to the side a bit, let my hands drop, lowered myself a few inches to get us on the same eye level, and nipped gently at his lower lip. I rolled my hips to hopefully entice him back into the moment.

"Thank you," he whispered.

I sucked on that lush lip of his, nothing touching him but my cock as it bumped over his hip bone. We both sucked in a short breath. I felt one hand settle on my side, then the other, as I toyed with his open mouth and rubbed against him.

"You make me wild," I confessed when his fingertips slid under my jacket. I pressed my fingers into fists to keep from being grabby.

"Same here," he replied, then yanked the back of my dress shirt free from my pants.

His hands slipped under the cotton fabric, his fingers bouncing off each rib. A rumble rolled from me. I covered his mouth with mine, probed as deeply as I could, eager for him to respond. He did, and it was glorious. His tongue stroked mine, inciting me to a frenzy. I pulled away from the kiss. He chased it, his grip on my ribs tightening. I let him catch my lips. He purred lightly when I lapped at his open mouth. Seemed he liked that, so I kept doing it, tonguing his lips and the corner of his mouth as he licked at my rapidly moving tongue.

"God, Adler," he moaned.

Something inside my brain broke hearing him hotly calling my name. I kissed him hard, my teeth skimming his. He grew a bit wild after that kiss. He shoved me and I instantly backed off. I didn't want to see anything but white-hot lust in those beautiful eyes of his.

"I'm sorry," I huffed. He shook his head, and then went to his knees, tugging at me to turn me. My shoulder blades kissed the locked door. "Shit, shit, shit," I growled when my fly was opened and my cock freed in one smooth-as-hell move.

Looking down. Nope. Should not have done that, but I had. Seeing him on his knees, his steely eyes heavy lidded as he took me into his mouth, almost did me in.

"Slow, Layton, please."

He bobbed his head but did not go slow. He sucked me hard and fast, using that tongue of his in ways that had me gasping and whimpering his name within seconds. God, he was good. *So* good...

"Layton... shit!"

I kept my eyes on him as I came. I dug my fingernails into the doorframe. He pulled me over the edge faster than any man ever had. He grabbed the silver-blue handkerchief from his breast pocket and spat into it, his gaze averted.

"You okay?" I asked between shudders and pants. He nodded, then got to one knee and pushed to his feet. He seemed uneasy now, his handkerchief wadded in his hand.

"I'm sorry... about this." He waved the handkerchief around.

"Dude, you're not the only man who doesn't swallow," I replied as I straightened back up to my normal height. He threw me a look that screamed that he thought I was placating him. "Seriously. Shit, I don't always, not all the time. It's fine."

I reached out to touch his cheek. He drew back a bit, then stepped closer, his eyes roaming over my face.

"Think I can do the same for you?" I cupped his cheek, then ran my thumb over his bottom lip. Man, his mouth was a work of art.

He looked like he was about to agree, and I was desperate to get my hands on him.

A knock on the door and an accompanying, heavily accented "Layton?" from Stan was enough to shake us free of the cloud of arousal that hung around us.

"Give me a moment," Layton called back.

"Lunch," Stan added.

"I brought my own," Layton said, all the while staring right at me. What was it with Stan? He seemed to be way too interested in what Layton was eating.

A very distinct sentence in Russian—saying what, who knew?—and then everything was quiet.

I looked at Layton with my most hopeful expression, but he shook his head. The moment was gone.

"You sure? I mean, you obviously need some relief, and I would love to get you into my mouth, among other things."

"No, no, not now. Later, maybe. Okay?"

"Sure, yeah, whenever you're okay for it." We were back to anxious Layton and sorely confused Alder status, which sucked. "Maybe we can go meet the guys?"

Oh-kay. That look was a for-sure no.

"Coffee, then? You and me? You do owe me a klatch."

"I have to watch social media, the phones…"

"You can take an hour; bring your phone."

He fumbled around for a reply. "I have to, uh… do something with this before we go." He lifted the hand holding the dirty handkerchief. No shit, I nearly jumped for joy just hearing him say he'd have coffee with me.

"Give it here." I opened my hand. Eyebrows knotted, he dropped the dirty square into my palm. I crammed it into my pocket, then reached around him. "Here, let me fix you up."

He watched as I opened the box and took out the perfectly folded handkerchief with the rainbow edging. I stepped close, eyes holding his, and slid the silky gift into his pocket.

"Now you look all sorts of hot." I plucked at the hankie, adjusting it a bit. He stole a kiss. It was nothing like the others we had shared, but it was just as powerful.

"Thanks for not being put off," he said.

"Thanks for finally taking my gift."

I let him step in to me. He began tucking my shirt back into place, his gaze flitting to touch mine several times as he worked on getting me presentable. Seemed that was his lot in life. Making Adler Lockhart presentable to the world. Lucky me.

"I'm, ah… what happened with us? I'm not sure about anything right now," he murmured as he tucked.

"I am. I'm sure we're going to get some coffee and celebrate you rocking the shit out of that presser. We might even get wild and have a muffin with our coffee." I gave him a wink, and he smiled. Pretty much right then I knew I'd fallen for him. When a man's little shy smile makes you feel like you lassoed the sun? You're already in freefall.

I DROVE us to this tiny little coffee shop about ten blocks from the barn. There were no hockey players in sight. Layton seemed okay with the place, although I felt cramped. It was tiny and trendy with little tables and retro seats that I knew would not hold my gigantic self.

"Are you going to sit down?" Layton asked as I stood balancing my coffee and a blueberry muffin.

"You think that spindly chair will hold me?"

He appraised it while cutting his muffin into four neat quarters. "It should. Things that look weak are sometimes stronger than you think."

"Wow, that was deep," I murmured, and cautiously lowered my weight downward. "Was that about chairs or you?"

He lifted his gaze from muffin-readying to me. "Both, maybe," he admitted.

"That's cool. So, here's the thing, okay. I like you. And I think you like me."

"Maybe."

I chuckled at his aloof reply. "That wild blowjob in your office suggests that you find me somewhat adorable."

"You're like an Irish setter," he blurted out, then returned to fussing over his muffin.

"You mean I'm bouncy, beautifully ginger, and I tend to bark before I think?" He gave me a coy smile, and what do you know, there was the sun again, shining into my soul. I was so done for. "Okay, I accept that. You always cut your muffin?"

"It's easier to keep under control that way."

He shook out a paper napkin with the coffee shop logo on it and placed it on his lap. I peeled the paper off my muffin and shoved the whole thing into my mouth. His eyes grew as round as the plate his quartered muffin sat on.

"This is how I control things," I managed to say around all the muffin.

He shook his head, then picked up one slice of his cranberry muffin. "That explains a lot," he said dryly, then nibbled on the edge of his muffin. It took me four tries to swallow. When I was able to breathe, I washed the glob of dough down with some really good coffee.

"Okay, so back to the thing," I said. "I like you and you like me. No, don't quibble. I'm still wobbly from the oral sex you perpetrated upon me."

He might have blushed just a little. A couple of women walked past us, chattering about kids. They sat down by the window. We'd chosen a more secluded spot by the counter. Layton had asked me to take the seat by the wall. He was checking his phone, his expression changing from smiling to angry and back again as quick as you could say internet idiots.

"I think we should date," I told him.

"You're not out," he keenly pointed out, placed his cell on the table, then took a tiny bite of muffin. "And even if you were, I'm not sure we should see each other. It's not professional."

"Okay, yeah, I'm not out, but I could be. I could reach over this table, grab you by the scruff of the neck, and kiss you right here in front of everyone walking up and down Susquehanna Street. Then I'd be out and that would be that."

"And I'd be left handling a situation that could be blown up into all the players on the Railers team turning gay overnight."

"Bullshit."

"You know it's true. And there would still be the fact that I work for the Railers management and you're a player."

"Was it not you that just put on that killer presser for a coach and a player?" I waved at the barista and asked for another muffin.

"That was different, and you just inhaled one muffin."

He sounded like my mother would if she'd ever cared about what I ate or when. It made me feel special.

"Getting great head always makes me hungry. You should see what I ingest after fucking pretty men with smoky eyes all night."

His bite of muffin froze an inch from his mouth. "You like talking dirty just to rattle me, don't you?"

"Yeah, I really do." I grinned as my second muffin arrived. I tossed a five at the server and told her to keep the change. "Back to us. I was thinking that maybe we'd just date once or twice a week. Movies and dinners mostly, because with our schedule more than that is about impossible."

"You're pretty presumptuous. I think I just said that we're not dating."

"No, you tossed out some silly rebuttal and I blew your lame argument out of the water."

His nose wrinkled. It was adorable.

Oh man, Adler, really, the saccharin level at this table is giving me diabetes and I'm just a voice in your head. Stop it, dude.

He lowered his fork with the muffin bite still on it. I saw the belligerence in his eyes. "I don't really appreciate you being so pushy. It's not an attractive trait and— Shit, now what?" He picked up his ringing cell and made the crinkled face again when he saw who was calling. I hoped to hell it wasn't someone calling to cuss him out over his work. But was he cute? Oh my God, yes.

"Mom, hi, I'm busy at the…" He rolled his eyes toward the ceiling. I took a bite of my second muffin and eavesdropped on the mother-son call.

"No, I haven't picked up anything for any of the kids yet."

I chewed as he deflected.

"Can we talk about Christmas dinner later? I'm doing

a coffee thing with a— Uh, well, he's a player for the Railers."

"I'm his date," I shouted.

He was not amused. "No, he's— Well, a date is a stretch. Serious? No. No, it's not serious because we're not — Bring him home for Christmas dinner? Ah, Mom, I'm not sure if that's—"

"I'd love to! Thank you, Mrs. Foxx!" I leaned on the table and yelled to make sure she heard me. Oh man, the look I got from Layton. It was simmering and sexy all at once. Just like he was. I chewed on my muffin as he stammered and tried to cook up some excuse. Guess Mrs. Foxx wasn't buying anything he said, and he ended the call looking like he'd sat on a hedgehog.

"That was out of line," he snapped. "You just can't invite yourself to my family's holiday!"

"First thing," I held up a finger, "I didn't invite myself. Your mother invited me, and I politely accepted." The furrows on his brow grew deeper. "Second thing," I added another finger and shook them at his cute nose, "it will be great. Do you have brothers and sisters? Nephews? Nieces? Oh man, is there a big tree? I bet there is. I'll have to go shopping. What does your mom like? I'll send Apollo to Cartier with a list. What?"

"You honestly cannot be *that* excited to spend Christmas with my family. It's loud and cramped, kids everywhere screaming and crying. It's not your thing at all, I'm sure."

"Sounds great! My Christmas memories are of me and the staff rattling around the Maine house until I went back to school. Loud and crazy sounds awesome."

He stared at me long and hard. "I'm sorry for that. It sounds lonely."

My last bite of muffin wedged in my throat. "It was

what it was. So, dinner tomorrow night? Dinner. A movie. More oral sex?" He seemed a little overwhelmed with me. "Should I tone down my inner setter a bit?"

"Maybe a little." He inhaled and let the breath go slowly. "Dinner is okay. No movie. We'll see about the oral sex."

Now it was time to smile so brightly *I* blinded *him*.

ELEVEN

Layton
___

I was up and out of my seat as soon as the plane landed. It's not that I hate flying—it gives me time to work uninterrupted—but the man next to me would not stop talking even though I'd given all the signals about how I didn't want to be disturbed. His Boston vowels grated on me as he waxed lyrical about the weather, politics, and every other boring thing he could think of.

He even handed me a business card. Real Estate, apparently; it figured.

Added to all that, I was tired and out of sorts, and I blamed Brady for it all. The oldest Rowe brother had made me go out for a beer, grilled me all night about how Ten was doing with the Railers, then proceeded to get me drunk. Not that it took much. Five beers I think, maybe more—I lost count.

I'd also drunk texted Adler, or Ad as I'd started to call him. It had been two weeks since that post-presser blowjob, and we hadn't actually done anything since that could be considered either sexual or very date-like.

He'd had an away stand, three games on the West

Coast. I'd been asked to go to Boston for a midweek meeting that had ended up lasting four days. We'd texted, but it had all been shallow stuff—comments on teammates from him, replies from me asking questions about how they were getting on back there.

Apart from the text I'd sent the night before, which he hadn't replied to.

I grabbed my overnight bag and walked as fast as I could away from the plane and through domestic arrivals, my mind far away from Boston or the annoying guy on the plane. All I could think about was how mortified I was by what I'd sent Ad. The Uber ride home was long enough for me to go through the stages of reaction to sending an inappropriate text.

First I re-read it.

I really need you to suck me off right now.

Then I read it one more time, like I had done a hundred times before. Just to make sure that what I thought I'd sent was actually there in black and white. Then I checked who I'd sent it to. I wasn't sure if it would be worse or better if I'd sent it to someone other than Ad.

What if I'd sent it to the team owner, or his PA? Imagine how much shit I'd be in if I'd sent that to the people who employed me.

But no. It had definitely gone to Ad.

I really need you to suck me off right now.

I groaned and covered my eyes. That was the second stage—the awful realization of what I'd done. I'd stepped way past considering dating a player. Clearly, when I was drunk and my libido took over, my need for a blowjob outweighed my professionalism.

The third stage was quicker each time. That moment I had to either wallow in embarrassment and regret, or accept that my brain needed to get on board with the idea of getting off in Ad's mouth.

I really wanted to touch him, and kiss him, and for him to suck me off. I was almost giddy with the excitement of a new attraction, and it was even worse because of what he'd done when we'd kissed.

He'd turned his body so he wasn't caging me. He'd known somehow that I didn't want to be trapped, and this was when the last stage of the whole thing hit me on the face.

I knew what I wanted physically, but the mental barriers were like iron around my heart. The last time I'd lusted after a jock, the only time before meeting Ad, had been a mess that I couldn't get out of my head. Despite counseling and the enormous support from my family, I was still fucked in the head and I knew it.

What if Adler held me down? What if he forced me to swallow? What if he shoved me onto all fours, then put his hands around my throat and used his body to hold me still as he fucked me? Raped me.

But what if he didn't do that? What if Adler Lockhart was the kindest lover I'd ever had, but then I had to tell him what had happened to me?

Then what?

"You okay?" The driver asked, glancing at me in the rearview mirror. I opened my mouth to say I was okay, then realized my hand was pressing my chest right over my heart and my breathing was rapid. "Hey! You need to go to the hospital?"

"No," I said, and dropped my hand and the cell I was gripping so hard in the other. "I'm fine."

The driver stared at me some more, to the point where I was concerned he wasn't watching his driving. Then, seemingly satisfied that I wasn't stroking out, he refocused on the road, and I attempted to relax.

After all those stages I came right around to the fact that any physical intimacy was off the cards with Ad. I needed to find my usual type—smaller, thinner, softer.

The driver looked me up and down and frowned as I paid, but at least he didn't ask me if I was okay, which was good, because in my head I'd gone right back to the first stage of shame over the text and was probably scarlet.

My place was on the third floor and I always took the stairs; someone with a sedentary career such as mine needed to get exercise in somewhere. When I rounded the last corner toward my door and saw Adler waiting for me cross-legged on the floor, I wasn't surprised. I should have been, but there was no room for surprise among the stress I was already fighting.

I stopped a few feet short of the door, and he stood up but didn't move toward me.

"That was some text," he said. His tone was careful, and I looked at him for the longest time, wondering if he was going to add anything else.

"I was drunk," I said finally.

"I guessed that."

I pulled out my key and let us both in, closing the door behind me and waiting with my back to the solid wood. Adler prowled my small apartment, stopping at the photos on the wall and examining them. Was he actually looking at them, or waiting for me to talk? He looked good in sweats and a Railers hoodie, his hands pushed deep into the pockets. His hair was unstyled, like he'd showered and not bothered to worry about adding product or fussing in front of a mirror.

"Have you been to practice today?" I asked.

I knew there was no game tonight, that they were

playing the Canes tomorrow, and that the game after that was against a Canadian team. That was as far as my knowledge of games went, although over the past couple of weeks I'd become quite proficient in some of the weird terms attached to the game itself. Jane had explained a lot as we'd watched the Railers last matchup against the LA Kings on the monitor in the video room.

We'd lost that one, or rather the Railers had lost in overtime on a lucky bounce. I wasn't entirely sure when I'd begun to consider myself part of the Railers team; it wasn't like I'd be employed by them past Christmas.

"Yeah," he said, and for a moment I wasn't sure what he was saying yes to, then I recalled that I'd asked about practice. "Spoke to Jane, asked her when you'd be back."

"How long have you been waiting?"

"An hour, maybe two. She knew the flight time, but I wanted to be sure to see you, so I got here early."

"You should have texted me and I would have—"

"Really?" he interrupted me sharply. "I should have opened my phone to text you and see what you sent me last night."

"I'm sorry about that," I apologized, hoping I didn't sound too miserable.

Ad pushed his hand through his soft hair, and it fell in layers over his forehead. He didn't say anything, but then he shrugged off his backpack and pulled something out before placing it on the coffee table. "I saw this and thought of you."

It was a mug in a box, and I could see the design from where I was standing. An Irish setter with a massive bone in its mouth stared out at me.

"I'm a bone hound," I said, and looked up from the mug to Ad.

"I know," he said. "It's inappropriate and non-PC and you can't take it to work with you, but it was funny, and after the whole setter thing it seemed right." He stopped and huffed. "Yeah, I know what you're thinking."

"What is it I'm thinking?" I wasn't sure I should ask him that; it felt like I was falling into a trap here.

"That I've learned nothing, and that I can't stop thinking about sex and you, or sex with you. And that it's a gift and you hate gifts."

I wasn't entirely sure what to broach first. Sex or gifts. Both were minefields. "You can't give me gifts."

"You took my handkerchief."

"I had to," I said, heat rising in my face. I still hadn't moved from the door, needing it to hold me up.

"Yeah, well, this is different," he said, and crossed to stand in front of me, less than a few inches separating us. He held out a hand, and I took it instinctively, and he tugged me closer, away from the door, pushing me gently until the backs of my legs hit the sofa.

"Sit down," he said softly.

I sat, and expected him to pace and talk, or maybe sit next to me, or anything but what he actually did.

With grace that belied his size, he went to his knees between my legs and rested his hands on my thighs. He looked up at me, his blue eyes filled with emotion.

"Adler?" I asked, or begged, or fuck if I know what I was saying or for what reason.

He leaned forward and pressed a kiss to the fly of my suit pants, nuzzling the erection that was growing fast. Then he unzipped me and urged me to raise my ass until he could pull pants and underwear down to my thighs. He stopped, considered the issue at hand, then clearly decided he wanted more. Between us, my shoes were off, my socks, and he opened my shirt, pressing kisses to my chest, focusing on each nipple for a short time before sitting back on his haunches and looking up at me again.

"When you texted me, you know what I did?"

"What?" I could hear the breathlessness in my voice and feel the way I was wriggling to get my cock closer to the hands he was loosely resting on my thighs again. His fingers traced patterns on my skin, and I'd never felt so exposed. He was fully dressed, and I was naked in the middle of the afternoon.

"I had my hand on my cock and I got myself off just to the images of what I could do to you. I imagined my mouth on you, my fingers pressing inside you, and I came so fucking hard."

"Ad—"

"May I?"

I'd lost my train of thought there. "May you what?"

"May I slick my fingers up and push inside you at the same time as sucking you off? Tell me it's okay?"

He looked pained, like he was expecting me to say no.

Fear snapped inside me, and I pushed it aside. I wasn't going to let my past dictate the here and now. Not with Adler.

"Please," I murmured.

He reached for his bag, pulled out lube, and slicked his fingers. As he took my cock in his mouth, sucking just the end then sliding down as far as he could, he pressed his fingers against my hole and massaged me there. I lifted a little, my cock pressing deeper into his mouth, and I apologized even as he groaned against me. He knew what he was doing, knew how I felt right at that moment. He pressed harder, and I moaned at the sensation of his fingers against me, his mouth hot and wet on my cock. This was every single fantasy I had and more. I wanted to touch him, but I didn't. Instead I curled my hands into the throw pillows that came with the sofa and tried to stop myself coming too fast.

Embarrassingly wanton.

He pushed my legs wider, the rhythm of his sucking and pressing his fingers inside, and me on the edge of everything, and then I couldn't stop myself. There wasn't even any warning as my orgasm hit me hard, and he took it all, looking up at me and giving the tip of my sensitive cock one last lick before sitting back on his haunches again with a smug, self-satisfied look on his face.

Ass.

He was getting himself off, sitting there with his hands pushed into his sweats, looking at me sprawled near-naked on my sofa, the afternoon sun weak through the large windows. When he came over his hand, he was still smiling.

But then the smile turned to something more, a thoughtful expression, before he sat up and kissed me.

I didn't even mind that he loomed over me, because I knew he wouldn't hurt me.

"Okay, okay," I said into the kiss. "I'll keep the damn mug."

SOMETHING CHANGED between us that day, and I know most of it was on me.

Even dealing with the vilest of emails and tweets from the most bigoted assholes I'd ever seen, I always had Adler's smile to think about. For every evil thing we received about Ten and Jared, we received a hundred supportive emails, and only ten people had said they wouldn't use their season tickets.

I suggested it would be good PR to refund them the

money. All Felix said was a very heated "Fuck 'em." I didn't broach the subject again.

Ad had left me more gifts; sometimes they were sitting on my desk, other times he handed them to me post-blowjob when I was at my most vulnerable. But they weren't expensive. Among others, I was now the proud owner of a Tennant Rowe bobblehead, an inflatable Stanley Cup that sat in the corner of my office, and a Railers tie with Adler's number on it.

I was also the proud owner of a brand-new offer from the Railers management; a full-time position with a view towards the team becoming a center of excellence and loaning me out to other teams. I'd told them I'd give them an answer when my contract was up in the new year. I was half excited and half terrified of accepting a role in a hockey team when the man I was falling for was always there.

The only other blip on the horizon was Christmas at home. Not that it was an issue for Adler; he was beyond hyped, and the gifts he'd been buying were all piled in the corner of his dining room. I saw them all on my one and only visit to his place.

The same night I met Adler's friend Apollo, and was aware that I was being silently judged by the man. We'd managed to get through an entire mug of coffee before Apollo had been more than direct with me.

"So you're the guy, then," he said. Which was an obvious statement to make, as Adler had introduced me as the man he was exchanging blowjobs and kisses with.

Freaking Adler and his lack of filter.

"Yeah," I said, which I hoped was the right answer.

Apollo nodded, made me another coffee, and offered me cake. Seemed that was all he'd needed to hear, because he launched into stories of when Adler was a kid, and threatened to get out an old photo album.

Adler was different around Apollo—calmer, franker, if that was possible, and so relaxed I thought he'd be falling asleep on the sofa.

"You want to see what I bought your family?" he asked me, and seemed more awake. He dragged me to the pile. The big pile. The enormous heap of things in embossed bags. I saw names like Cartier, Tiffany, Prada and Ralph Lauren.

"Adler, this is too much," I said, and felt like a bastard when Adler's face momentarily fell. The smile that came back was a little forced.

"I wasn't sure what to get," he said in explanation. "I'm going to wrap everything tonight, or at least Apollo and I will, and then get them shipped to your address."

"Adler—"

He stopped me with a kiss, then hugged me. "Please let me. I need them to know the sort of man I am, and how much it means to me that they invited me."

We were flying to Michigan the day after his final pre-Christmas game against the Blue Jackets, and that gave me some time to warn my family that Adler was a millionaire who liked buying things, and that they shouldn't feel uncomfortable.

I hoped my family would be able to rise above it and see the gifts for what they were. Not that the kids would care, particularly given the new game consoles and games I spotted right at the back.

There was more to these presents than a man spending his money. I saw something in Adler. A desperate need to be wanted and liked that I'm not sure anyone else apart from Apollo was aware of.

So I did what felt right. I pulled Adler in for a close hug and told him how much everyone would love the gifts.

When his smile became more natural again, I knew one thing.

I'd done the right thing.

TWELVE

Adler

It's the weirdest sensation sitting in a rink that had been your home away from home for four years, watching a homage to you on the Jumbotron, while wearing a different team's jersey. The short video compilation during a TV timeout was a good one. Highlights of my four years with Columbus, lots of replays of goals I'd made and celebrations with Columbus players, many of whom I still called friends and would for years. When the homage was over, the fans stood and clapped. I lifted my stick to the people of Columbus in thanks. I'd liked my time there. It was a good organization and a great city with strong hockey love pumping through its veins. When I'd been traded, it had hurt, I'll be honest. But a professional athlete is a commodity, we all know that. Hell, even The Great One had been traded, but it still stung.

My first couple of weeks in Harrisburg had been manageable only because of Apollo being there and doing all the shit-work a move encompassed. I'd just jumped on a plane and started playing hockey like the good boy I am.

I'd spent lots of time comparing the two cities and found them to be equal in all ways. Then Layton Foxx entered my life and Harrisburg had brightened considerably. Now I couldn't imagine being anywhere else, but Columbus and its great fans would always hold a spot in my heart. That didn't mean I wasn't going to try to beat the shit out of my old team. It was a point of pride. A sort of tweak of their noses to score on them as often as I could. Okay, it was a loud "neener, neener, neener" in my most childish inner voice.

I might have actually tossed that taunt at my old goalie, Steve Willis, after I deflected a blistering snap shot from Tennant Rowe into the net. I could see Steve's green eyes narrow before I skated off to hug my line mates.

Yeah, I was just that immature at times.

Seated on the bench after the fourth Railers goal, my mind left the game just for a second. It was okay, since we were up by two goals with less than ten minutes in the third period. Plans for the next few days bounced around inside my head. I had to leave as soon as I could to get to Harrisburg. The team was pulling out in the morning, but I wanted to get home tonight and get a few hours of loving-Layton time before we left for Michigan, where there would be no loving-Layton time. I'd even gone as far as having a Lockhart jet sent to the John Glenn International Airport here in Columbus to whisk my ass back to Pennsylvania with all due haste.

"What the fuck?!" shouted every Railer, as well as the coaching staff.

I jerked back to the game, my gaze flying to the big screen over the ice. There I saw a replay of Stan being knocked off his skates as one of the big Columbus defenseman crashed the crease. There was a big knot of players pushing and shoving as Stan struggled to get to his skates. Stan made a beeline toward the linesman who'd been behind the net. Much yelling took place, most in loud Russian and directed at the man in black and white who was still indicating that it was a good goal.

Stan went back to his net and shoved it to the boards. Our bench was irate. Our captain was livid. Our head coach immediately challenged the goal, stating that there had been goaltender interference. When the decision came back that there had been no goaltender interference, things got a little vibrant on the Railers bench. Coaches were screaming at refs, refs were yelling at coaches, our captain was berating a linesman, and Stan lost his shit. I sat there amid the chaos and watched the towering Russian whip the ever-loving shit out of his net, his fat paddle of a stick shattering as he pummeled the pipes.

After that little fiasco, we lost our momentum. Columbus rallied and socked another one past Stan, this one scored while I was on the ice. Not a good thing. We went to overtime, which pissed me off because of the whole jet sitting on tarmac situation. Tennant Rowe pulled me aside before the five minutes of four-on-four began.

"We need to end this fast," he said as we took a breather at the bench for another TV break. "I'm going to try to get it to you right after the faceoff. Don't be fancy, okay? I know you're known for the pretty stuff, but pretty stuff right now is going to get us a loss."

"I'll only do pretty if it's needed," I assured my center.

We gathered around for the faceoff. Tennant won it clean by tapping it between the Columbus center's legs, then raced around the man to pick up his own pass. There was lots of room on the ice, so when the crisp pass from Ten near the boards settled on my stick, I took off at center ice and never looked back. No fancy stuff, just straight at the goalie, a deke left and then right, making Steve move with me. He got bold and went too far wide, which opened the net, and I socked it in.

I threw myself into the glass near the Columbus goal as the red light flashed. My old fans gave me the finger at the same time my new teammates leaped on me and started pounding my helmet. Beating my old team was a fine Christmas present. Not as good as the one I hoped to give Layton when I got home, though.

The only tiny hitch in the perfect night was Stan coming up to me before the press arrived and asking about Layton's eating habits. I assured the goalie that he was fine, and he loped off, appeased. It stuck in my craw, though. Who the shit was Stan to be asking about Layton? *Why* was Stan asking about Layton? Were they hooking up? Did he know Layton and I were hooking up? How? Did they whisper about me after they had sex? Laugh at me, call me a disappointment…

A nugget of jealousy glowed bright and green in my breast. Then sanity returned. No. Layton and Stan were not hooking up. Stan was just being nice. Yeah. That was it. It had to be, because if it was something else, I'd have to pound the stuffing out of my own goalie, and that might cause a bit of a problem with team spirit and all.

I pushed through the postgame stuff, showered, dressed, and grabbed a cab after quick rounds of "happy holidays" with the team. The Lear 45 XR was right where it was supposed to be. A lovely young woman employed by CKAL—my father's mergers and acquisitions consulting company—greeted me warmly with a smile and a cocktail. Being the A in CKAL had its benefits. We were in the air within seconds, me with a tall glass of imported beer in hand and a lovely woman to converse with. Tracy—that was her name—served me a massive platter with some of the biggest shrimp I'd ever seen and a large dish of cocktail sauce. I sent a cryptic text to Layton as I eyed the feast in front of me.

My place. 2 am. Bring your appetite for all things delicious.

In little over an hour I was back in Harrisburg and on my way home. Apollo greeted me in the living room.

"What are you doing here?" I asked, hands filled with a large silver platter covered with gigantic prawns.

"I live here, remember?" he answered as he sauntered past with a pile of clean clothes. "I'm packing your bag for your trip."

"Dude," I said as I followed him to my bedroom. "You didn't have to do that. I can pack my own bags."

"No, you really can't."

He gently placed shirts and slacks into the titanium multi-wheel suitcase sitting open on my bed. It had been a birthday gift from Karrie Anne. She'd sent it over from Europe last year. The gift had been there for my birthday, but not her.

"I've also arranged for a car to pick you up from the airport and deliver you and Mr. Foxx to his mother's house in Alton Heights. You're free from engagements for two days, but need to be back here for a Friday night game against Philadelphia. I also watered the spider plant and dusted."

"You rock. Is there anything I can do for you?"

He gave me some side-eye. "Try coming in your hand. The number of dirty handkerchiefs in the wash has tripled since you and Mr. Foxx became friends."

"Layton doesn't like to swallow."

He rolled his eyes. "Far too much information. But I

did pack about twenty clean handkerchiefs for your trip." He closed the case, latched it, and turned to look at me. "Ad, do me a favor, okay? Try to keep a rein on yourself."

"I know, you already told me not to buy anyone any more presents." I shuffled the shrimp from one hand to the other.

"Yeah, there's that, but I see how much you love this man."

"I never said that. Never. Not once. Did I?" I didn't recall saying the L-word in any way that was linked with Layton.

"You didn't have to. It's written all over your face. Mr. Foxx is nice and very good-looking but deeply troubled. Don't let your desire to be loved override what he can give you, okay?"

"Yeah, sure, okay. I'll go slow. I promise."

"You don't mean a word of that, I know." He sighed, padded over to me, and gave me a chaste kiss on the lips. I wiggled the prawn platter out of the way. "I'm leaving now. I want to get home, sleep, and be able to do Christmas Eve Mass with my parents."

"Cool. Tell them I wish them the best holiday ever. Seems funny not to be going with you this year."

"It's nice that you have someone else in your life now. Just don't suffocate the man, okay?" He patted my cheek, snuck a shrimp from under the plastic wrap, and walked off.

I heard the doorbell ring. My body reacted instantly knowing it was Layton on the other side of the door. It had been days since I'd last seen him. When I opened it he looked so good. Relaxed, calm, smiling, casually dressed.

"Missed you," I said as his gaze moved over me then settled on the shrimp platter. "Treats for later. Come in. May I kiss you?"

"Sure," he said as he slipped in around me. I leaned in, stole a tiny smooch, then jumped back out of the way when Apollo came charging at us with travel bags bouncing off his back.

"Hello, Mr. Foxx." He smiled at Layton, then wagged a finger at me as he hurried past. "You, remember what I said. Have fun. Merry Christmas, Ad, Mr. Foxx."

"Same to you," Layton said before I closed the door on my best friend. "He doesn't like me."

"He does."

"He calls me Mr. Foxx."

"Tell him he can call you Layton, then."

"Is that what he's waiting for?" Layton looked bemused.

"He's protective, is all. Worried about me falling for you too quickly. He seems to think I can't control myself for some reason."

"Your lack of a filter might have something to do with how he thinks," Layton said, then lifted the shrimp platter from my hands. "Why don't we put these in the fridge? Warm seafood makes me nervous."

I followed him into the kitchen. He pulled open the refrigerator and slid the platter onto a shelf.

"I have the jet waiting at Harrisburg International," I said. "I thought we could have some sex, eat some shrimp, grab a nap, then fly to Michigan."

"Wait, what?" He closed the fridge and turned to look at me. "What jet?"

"The one I hopped on to get home early."

I took a few steps closer to him, because I really wanted to get all over him right now. He folded his arms over his chest, the dark gray sweater really working with his eyes.

"It's a Lear. One of about fifteen in the CKAL corporate fleet. It's cool. I do it all the time. Cole doesn't care."

"I already bought airline tickets. Ad, you can't just change plans at the last minute. I have everything worked out. I gave you a copy of the itinerary."

"I'll reimburse you for the plane tickets. You worry too much about details."

I closed in on him, and he stiffened visibly. Maybe he was mad about the spontaneity of my actions, or maybe he was feeling pressured. I took a few steps in reverse. He still looked rattled, so I pushed my hands into my front pockets.

"Layton, this is a trip home. Why do we need an itinerary?"

"Because you have to keep things in life under control!" he barked. I gaped at him. His eyes flared, then he looked away from me. "Okay, that was not good. I'm sorry, Adler. I just... when you do this unscripted stuff it mildly freaks me out."

"Mildly?"

He sighed. "Maybe more than mildly," he confessed.

I reached out tentatively to touch his collarbone. His baggy sweater had slid off his shoulder a bit, and there it was, that sexy bone hiding under his kissable skin. He didn't jerk or grow more anxious. He just stood there in front of my fridge, allowing me to stroke his collar bone.

"I'm sorry for being so unruly," I said, which pulled a shaky smile from him. My finger traveled up the side of his neck. His eyelashes lowered and his head tilted to the side as he exhaled long and steadily. "I love the way you feel. May I feel more of you? I really need to do that, Layton."

"Sure, yes, please."

I got him naked right there in the kitchen, his clothes thrown over the island and counters. He melted into me, pliable and needy, just like I was. His mouth was hot, his skin sweet. I touched and then I licked, falling to my knees, tasting his cock and balls, then gently persuading him to turn, bend over the counter and offer me his ass. His acquiescence was timid and slow, but he did as I asked and I tried not to press into him too hard. He could still get away if he needed to. God above, he was beautiful spread out in front of me so trustingly. My hands shook just a bit as I massaged his tight ass cheeks. He tensed when my tongue flickered over his hole, the tension disappearing when I lapped hungrily at his ass. He trembled and groaned. I wet a finger and pressed it into him, taking his balls into my mouth.

"I need more," he panted, his skin making a squeaking noise as his upper half writhed on the countertop. I gave him more. More sucking, more stroking his sweet spot, more of everything that I could give him right now. I so wanted to fuck him. Like this. Him gyrating around, skin stuck to the counter, me behind him, pulling his hair as I pounded into him like a man possessed.

"You close?" I asked between long, sloppy, wet tastes of his ass. A gargling sound rolled out of him that might have been a yes. I reached between his legs, found his prick, and gave him several strokes, making sure to twist my hand over the head each time. He blew apart loudly, rolling his hips to get my tongue deeper into his ass.

"Ah shit," he groaned as I milked him, cum coating my fingers. His legs folded a little, the counter catching most of his weight. My own release was just a stroke away, his spunk and mine slippery and slick on my right hand. I nipped at his ass cheeks, nuzzled them, kissed each firm globe softly. Then I stood up and leaned my hips into his ass, my still-hard cock settling between his cheeks. He inhaled sharply, his body tightening.

"It's okay, babe," I murmured against his skin. "I just want to feel you under me. Nothing more happens, I swear."

"Ad…" he panted. "I— Shit…"

"It's just me, Adler. I won't hurt you. You're safe with me."

He shuddered deeply. I trailed my fingers over his ribs. I bent over his back, dropping kisses along his spine and shoulders until I reached the nape of his neck. There I peppered the fine, dark hairs with light kisses. He lay there under me, soft and supple, his breathing slowing, taut muscles loosening.

"You are a magnificent man. Strong, brave, smart," I whispered beside his ear. "I adore you."

He craned his head to the side, his smoky eyes still aglow with passion. I kissed his neck hungrily to keep myself from uttering what Apollo had told me not to utter even though I felt that L-word bursting to life in my breast. Maybe now would be a good time to suggest eating some shrimp.

———

THE LIMO WAS a wee bit out of place as it cruised the lower-to-middle-class neighborhood Layton had grown up in. He seemed out of sorts and edgy when we pulled up to his mom's house. I tried to pull him out of the weird place he was in, but he seemed resigned to being aloof. I let him be simply because my nerves were shot. I needed this family to like me, because I was crazy about their son.

The tiny Foxx home in Alton Heights was packed tight with people. Lots of people, all resembling Layton, who were trying to peer through my flesh to see inside me. I did my best to be funny, charming Adler, the guy everyone likes because he's so clever and laid back. The one who, according to Layton, needed a filter. Maybe I shouldn't be that Adler. Maybe I needed to be a less rambunctious

Adler. I tamped down the need to tell the Foxx family a really funny joke Arvy had passed along a few days ago.

I shook hands with a Zach, an Oscar, an Eden and a Jack. Then I smiled and thanked Mrs. Foxx for letting me come. I wished I had my gifts in hand to shove at them, but they were already here somewhere according to USPS delivery tracking. Maybe the distrustful looks would ease up if they could open gifts. Kids shouted and bounced off the walls. Layton stayed by my side, working his bottom lip, as we made our way into the living room. I was tense. Something stupid was on the tip of my tongue.

Then I saw the tree. It was lopsided and had a hole in the middle. Someone had stuffed a raggedy Santa doll into the gap. The lights weren't evenly strung, the ornaments were all handmade by kids and grandkids, and the angel had a bent wing and a crooked halo. The presents under it weren't stacked for eye appeal, and included mine. It was a disreputable tree and would not even have been granted admittance to any of the Lockhart homes. I loved it instantly and ran to it to scope out every ornament up close.

"No kidding." I grinned and plucked a paper nutcracker from one of the boughs. A young Layton had colored, cut out, and glued the nutcracker onto an empty toilet paper roll. His name was scribbled on the big, bent hat. I held the ornament up. Layton looked pinched. "Okay, seriously, this is adorable! How old were you when you made this?"

"I don't know. Six or seven, maybe," Layton said, his huge family circling like sharks. Mrs. Foxx settled in beside Layton protectively. I got where they were coming from. If what I assumed had happened to Layton had really happened, I'd be overprotective too.

I turned the ornament around slowly, admiring it. "I

remember making something like this… it was a reindeer, though, in first grade. We all made one for our parents. I took all kinds of care with it on the trip home, making sure it never got bent on the flight or in the limo. No, it was second grade. Yeah, that was the year Cole and Karrie Anne went to Rome for the holidays. Yep. I ended up giving it to Apollo's folks. They put it on their tree next to something Apollo had made. I don't think it ever made it to the tree in the grand foyer at home. Huh. Guess it wasn't good enough."

Layton reached out to lay a hand on my forearm. I started a bit, then flushed. I jammed the nutcracker back in place. When I worked up the courage to look at him, his gaze held all kinds of things.

"It was good enough, Ad." He gave my arm a light squeeze.

"Brunch is ready," Mrs. Foxx said, her gray eyes a little bit warmer,.

Brunch was a big bowl of scrambled eggs, tiny little breakfast sausages, and a pile of toast. Jelly was in jars. Butter wasn't butter but margarine in tubs, and the kids sat at the table with the adults and talked non-stop. The meal was sloppy, loud, and not at all refined. I fucking loved it. One of Layton's brothers asked me about hockey. Another asked me about my childhood. His sister enquired about my past relationships. I was about to reply to her when Layton steamrolled me.

"This is going to stop now," he barked, then slammed his fork on the table. The kids fell into silence, as did the adults. I sat back all kinds of shocked. "He's here as my guest. He's not here as a suspect to a crime. He's the man I'm dating."

"Son, we're just concerned about you," his mom said.

Layton threw his mom a dark look, then pushed to his feet. "I need some air." He stalked out of the room.

I sat there with my mouth open and a breakfast link on my fork, staring at the empty seat beside me. Wow. What was the deal with Layton and his mom? My lover had a shitload of secrets.

"I— Ah… I'll go talk to him," I said as the front door slammed.

I shoved the sausage into my mouth, left the packed dining room, grabbed my coat and a sprig of plastic mistletoe that had been tacked to a doorway, and jogged out into the bitter cold. A tiny snowflake drifted downward, then another. I spied Layton heading west, his gait rapid. I ran after him. He tossed me a glower when I stepped up beside him. He looked cold in his thin sweater. I draped my coat around his shoulders.

"You'll get cold," he said.

"I'm a hockey player. Cold won't kill me."

We pounded the pavement in silence for a few minutes until we came to the end of the block. I danced around him, stepping in front of him and blocking his path. Snow was piled up on either side of the walk and I knew he wouldn't step out into the foot-high banks. Not with those shiny loafers he had on. I dangled the mistletoe over his dark head. He gave the green bunch a glare that should have incinerated it. I wanted to ask about the looks he'd exchanged with his mom, but he needed to feel safe enough with me to tell me. Guessed we weren't there yet, but we would be.

"What are you doing?"

"I'm claiming a Christmas kiss. It's tradition." I wiggled the plastic clump. A cold wind blew down the street. Fuck, it was icy.

"Adler, stop being an ass." He glanced around me. "Now get out of the way. I need to process my shit."

"Uh, sorry, no. Not moving. I don't think you can make me, so just give me my kiss and we'll go back home. Where it's warm."

"You're a hockey player. You don't get cold." He snuggled into my coat, the sexy prick.

"I was thinking of you," I countered. A flake landed on his head. It was sparkly and perfect for a second before it melted into his thick hair.

"Uh-huh. Alder, this is stupid. You're not out. We're standing on the corner of Wisteria and Crocus Lanes at noon on Christmas Eve day. Everyone is home and probably peeking out their windows at us." He waved a hand at the houses surrounding us. "There's no way you're kissing me here on the corner, so stop with the asinine holiday shit and move so I can walk off some of this—"

I kissed him. Right there on the corner of Wisteria and Crocus Lanes in Alton Heights, Michigan. And I mean I *kissed* him. My arm went around his waist, I jerked him into me, and I kissed him so hard and so long there could be no doubt in the mind of any Michigander spying on us that we were a couple.

When the kiss ended, he stumbled back a step, his eyes hot and confused and his lips wet and pink from the pressure of my mouth on his.

"Guess that means I'm coming out now," I told him, my hand with the mistletoe dropping to my side. I wasn't cold anymore. Amazing what kissing the man you loved could do for your internal thermostat.

"Are you sure about this?" he asked breathlessly, his words steaming in front of his face.

I bobbed my head. "You need me to kiss you again to prove it?" I hoisted the mistletoe back up in the air.

He shook his head. Then he nodded. So I kissed him again. And I kept kissing him, under that plastic ball of green leaves and white berries, every time I could for the entire time we were in Michigan. Mrs. Foxx gave me the mistletoe clump when we left, and a hug, so that I could keep kissing her son when we were back in Harrisburg. I didn't need mistletoe to do that—I planned on kissing Layton every day for the rest of my life if he'd have me.

THIRTEEN

Layton

I was expecting Adler, so didn't hesitate in calling for the person knocking on my door to come in. Since coming back from Michigan, he'd just been there all the time. Staying over with me, kissing me, loving on me, and bit by bit he was cracking the shell around my heart. We hadn't made it super obvious that we were a couple here at the rink, but if I turned a corner at the arena and he was there, then you can bet your bottom dollar there was kissing.

I smiled up as the door opened, but it wasn't Adler standing there with that damn mistletoe in his hand. Nope, it was Mr. 69 himself, Dieter Lehmann, left wing and all-around sex god if I recalled our first meeting.

"Do you have a few minutes?" he asked, edging into the room like there was a dragon inside and he didn't want to be spotted. This wasn't the Dieter I was used to, not the brash skater who had just turned twenty-five and who had to make a deliberate effort not to say something that was politically incorrect. He'd been the easiest to talk to about the implications of his words for the team, and for himself, but he also seemed to forget them as soon as he walked out the door. I wasn't entirely sure he was listening to me; he often looked like his mind was elsewhere. He was a very good hockey player, or so I'd been told, someone who had worked away in the lower levels of the hockey leagues, the AHL, in the team that fed new talent to the Railers. He skated on what I now knew was the fourth line, and he was up with the Railers covering injury.

"Of course," I said.

He stepped in fully and shut the door behind him. "Shit," was all he said, not moving from the door, still gripping the handle, his knuckles white. This wasn't good—this was distinctly bad, and I had a horrible feeling that my already shitty day was going to get worse.

"Sit down," I said, and gestured to the chair, into which he collapsed so hard that it squeaked in protest. "Are you okay?" I asked, even though what I really wanted to say was, "What have you done now?"

"I think things are… not good." He searched for those final two words so hard that his face creased with a deep frown. Surreptitiously, I pulled my notebook in front of me and picked up the Montblanc pen that I had taken to using now, much to Adler's glee.

"How are things not good?"

"She's only doing it because stupid Ten and stupid Coach decided to spread their big gay love."

My back stiffened as Dieter held up his hands when he spoke. He was agitated; shock had clearly given way to anger of sorts. Whatever. No man got to sit in my office and act like he was entitled to debate Ten and Jared's choices.

"Shit," he snapped, and scrubbed his eyes. He had very nice eyes; I'd noticed that in our last meeting, green and amber that at the moment were dull with misery. "I didn't mean that how it sounded," he said, and shuffled in the chair. Dieter certainly wasn't the biggest on the team, but the chair was under a lot of strain.

The door opened and Adler stepped in without knocking and with a cheerful "Hey, sexy". I looked from him to Dieter and back again.

Dieter's eyes widened.

"I'll be out in a bit," I explained to Adler, who backed right out looking apologetic. Only when the door closed did I look back at Dieter, who was staring right at me.

"You and…"

"Yeah."

"Cool."

That was that—someone on the team other than me and Adler knew about us. Baby steps, I guessed. "So tell me what happened."

I think the interruption was a good thing, as Dieter seemed calmer.

"My ex has a video, and stills, and she thinks I'll pay her off."

"She's blackmailing you."

Dieter shook his head. "Yeah, and I'm worried the photos will get out and," he paused again, clearly searching for the right words, "cause embarrassment," he finished.

"Okay." I swallowed back the anxiety. This was my job and I could do it well. I scribbled some notes on my pad. "So what are these photos? Are we talking you covered up, in bed, or more explicit?"

He wrinkled his nose and looked at anything but me. "It's me in bed, yeah. Well, on the bed actually, to start with at least. Then there's video, of me off the bed, and um… yeah."

"There's more?"

"Well, she's taking the video of me with the third we had in bed with us. A guy."

I glanced up from my notes, a hundred questions in my head, not sure how to frame what I thought about Dieter at that moment.

He muttered something under his breath. "I was with the guy, okay, and I can see this undermines what you're doing here. I get that, and I'm sorry."

Oh. That was interesting.

"You identify as bi, then," I said, and made a note.

"I identify as liking sex, all kinds of sex, but I'm not an addict." He added the last bit with absolute conviction. "So she can't accuse me of that, because she was part of it as well."

"We can handle this if it gets out," I reassured him. How I was going to handle it, I didn't know, but the challenge was there and I felt calm and centered. "I'll need to have all the information you can get. Okay?"

Dieter nodded. "Thanks," he said, and stood. "I'll get everything I can."

"Don't pay her," I warned.

"I won't unless I have to," he said.

That wasn't completely what I wanted to hear, but it was a start. Last thing I needed was to have to battle blackmail as well as a threesome on camera.

He was still standing there.

"Is there anything else?"

He slumped back into the chair and this time he buried his head in his hands. What could be worse than a sex tape?

"I am an addict," he said through his hands.

"A sex addict," I said, summarizing where I thought we were in this conversation. I could deal with this; there were things we could do.

"No," he lifted his face and I was startled to see his eyes bright like he was trying not to cry. "Pain medication."

I didn't know what to say, and I knew I was sitting there like an idiot. I really needed to get a grip.

"You want to tell me?"

"No," Dieter said, with complete honesty. "But I guess I have to. No one here knows, it's not public record, I'm clean now, working hard to stay that way, but you need to know what else could come out."

"This girlfriend…"

"Marianne."

"Marianne knows about the meds."

He looked at me and he seemed so lost. "I don't know."

This I could handle. "Okay, anything that happens, we can deal with it."

"Really?" He brightened, like I'd just handed him a million dollars.

"You need to talk to me though, keep telling me how you're doing."

"Okay," he stood up and extended his hand and we shook again. "Thank you."

I locked up my office after Dieter left, finding Adler in our usual meeting spot. We kissed quickly, then I took his hand and faced him head on.

"Management has offered me a position here full-time. I'd like to take it."

I wanted to add a question, like, "What do you think of that?" Even ask for his approval, like, "Is that okay?" I didn't need to when his lips curved in a smile that made his blue eyes spark.

"That's good news," he said. Then he kissed me, pulling me back into the shadows of the corridor. Anyone could walk past, but I didn't care. I had purpose here, and I had Adler, and I felt good.

Like nothing from my past could touch me.

———

STAN'S NEW Year party was like nothing I'd seen before. Apparently New Year is a big thing in Russia, and he opened up his large house to everyone on the team. I wasn't the best person at parties, never the life and soul, and I generally ended up in the kitchen. Let's be honest, if it had just been me then I would have made excuses.

But I was with Adler, who wanted to dance and mingle and joke, and through it all he was dragging me around. The party was team only, and although some of the team looked at our joined hands, no one actually called us out on it.

Until Mikhail arrived.

He was Stan's friend from their KHL time in Russia, and a Flyer, which apparently meant he was open for all catcalls and derogatory sarcasm. None of which appeared to faze him, because he gave as good as he got. He was a tall guy—way taller than a lot of people in the room; more a basketball player if I'd been asked to guess—which was where my problems started.

He was loud as well; had this booming laugh that I found just a bit too much. He was in the kitchen when I managed to get a break from the chaos in the main room, and at first I thought about turning around and leaving.

"Hello," he said, in less accented Russian than I'd come to expect from Stan.

Stan tried really hard with his English, but he'd picked up some pretty awful phrases that he used at any given moment. I tried to explain to him when things he used in a sentence weren't completely appropriate, but he just grinned at me, the big idiot.

"Hey," I said, and opened the huge fridge in search of a drink. I didn't really drink a lot of alcohol—always too much of a control freak, I guess. Which explained why I'd fallen asleep after three sips of eggnog on Christmas day.

I shut the door, jumping a mile when Mikhail was right the fuck there, smiling at me.

"Jesus," I cursed, and stumbled back and away.

He held up a hand in apology. "My bad."

"It's fine," I said.

"When you come and sort Flyers?" he asked.

"Sort ?"

"I think everyone on Railers is gay," he announced, and I bristled a little. Not everyone was gay—just me, Adler and Ten, and Jared and Dieter were bi. "We have gay man on team. He is scared," Mikhail added. "He like friend."

He stepped forward even as I moved back, until I couldn't move any further, my ass against a cupboard. With hindsight I was sure I would realize that Mikhail wasn't trying to intimidate me, or loom over me, or any one of a million triggers that were causing the tightness in my chest. But right now, my back was against the wall, I was trapped in the corner, and I really didn't fucking like it one bit.

"I'll give you my number," I said, and sidestepped a little, gauging how I could get past the big Russian and through the door to the party beyond. He crossed his arms over his chest and just stood there.

Okay, was this some Russian thing, standing still and looking all brooding and sulky?

"Excuse me," I said, my mouth dry. This was stupid. "I need to find Adler."

"Lockhart? I like him," Mikhail said. "Fast on ice. I feel bad I knocked him into glass at our last game, but feel good I caught him." He grinned like he'd made a joke, and he probably had, but his delivery was a little stilted.

"Uh-huh," I said, and straightened as the door opened and Adler came strolling in like he had all the time in the world. He stopped dead by the door and looked at the two of us—the tall, hulking Russian and his much smaller boyfriend who probably looked like a rabbit in a trap.

He was by my side in an instant, casually putting himself between me and Mikhail, holding my hand.

"Petrov, you fucker," he said with a smile in his voice, and held out a fist to bump.

"Lockhart," Mikhail said, and bumped him back. "You still got one past me."

"Stan has vodka out," Adler said, and Mikhail's face brightened, and within seconds it was just the two of us left in the kitchen. The huge kitchen that felt way too small.

"Come on," Adler said. He tugged my hand and went through a laundry room that had another door that opened into the front hall. From there he led me up the stairs, then seemed to consider which room he needed.

"I'm not doing this," I said, and tugged at his hand. "We're not getting off in Stan's place."

He gave me a look that said I was being an idiot and opened a door with a flourish. As soon as we stepped inside, he shut us in and walked to the wide patio doors, which he opened enough for the winter air to rush in. I inhaled in one greedy gulp and took the blanket that Adler handed me. He'd taken it from the bed, and it was thick, like a comforter.

"I stayed here one night before a game, when Apollo was away. Needed the company. How awesome is this room?"

The question was rhetorical, but I nodded and gave him a smile. I was tense, and hated feeling that way.

"This way," he said, and pulled me out onto the small patio, taking his own blanket. The night was inky black, and there wasn't a view as such, just the mass of trees that screened this beautiful house from the road. But the air was clear, and cold, and I needed the open space. We sat on recliners next to each other, and he moved his closer so we could lean on each other.

In silence, we sat for the longest time, until the fear in my chest subsided and all was left was absolute peace.

Adler did that for me.

And right there and then, I knew I'd fallen in love.

So he needed to know everything. It wasn't fair that this thing we had happening between us should keep going when I had all these secrets inside me.

I cleared my throat. "So, when I was seventeen I was dating this boy on the football team. Oliver, his name was. He was a catch—you know, a jock. Not out, but still he looked at me and saw something he wanted, and I was flattered. I was a typical nerd—big on math, bound and determined to be the first of my siblings to go to college. I fell big time for Olly, and in my head it was hearts and flowers."

Adler unwrapped a hand from his blanket and reached over, finding my hand in the folds of my cover and holding it tight. A brief rush of cold was a welcome balm for my overheated skin.

"I'm here," he murmured, but he didn't need to say a thing. He was by my side, but he was also buried deep in my heart, where I sometimes imagined I would like to keep him forever.

"He was part of the bullying I had to go through on a

daily basis, but I ignored that because he would give me these secret smiles, like he didn't mean to hurt me."

"Shit."

"Things went bad quickly. Word got out that he wasn't into girls as much as he needed to be—you know the sort of pressure jocks are under at school, right?"

"Yeah, but why do I feel like you're excusing this Olly guy for something?"

I squeezed his hand. "I'm not. It wasn't his fault, not really, but what his friends did… that was something else altogether. I was at a party; they spiked my drink. I woke up naked and on the side of the road. I don't remember what happened. I went home." Such a simple story for what had been a treacherous walk along a highway to my home.

I stopped, because it hadn't been that simple. When I'd woken up I'd been covered in blood from various cuts, there had been more than enough evidence that I'd been raped, and there had been photos of me on my phone, which they'd left next to me. I hadn't seen them until three days after the incident, when I'd finally charged the phone. Not enough of them had showed who had hurt me, just that it hadn't been only one person.

"Please…" Adler said, his voice thick with emotion. Was he saying I should carry on or stop? I didn't know. So I carried on, because I'd started now, and this needed saying.

"My brother found me in the front yard, took me inside, and I don't remember a lot of what happened. The cops came, took my statement, took samples. A doctor was called, I was torn, and the shame of it all… like I was a piece of meat everyone wanted to test and poke at." I couldn't go on for a second, and I glanced sideways at Adler, wondering what I would see.

Naked anguish and eyes bright with tears. I'd put that intense feeling there, and I felt so sorry that I was doing this to him, but he needed to know it all before what we had could go any further.

"What happened?" he asked, his voice broken.

"There wasn't enough to accuse anyone. I didn't have any memories. There was Rohypnol in my system, and I was over reasonable alcohol limits, although I don't recall drinking much. The cops tried—there were even some photos, but nothing helpful. When they finally found someone, a friend of Oliver's, he denied everything and was acquitted. I finished school at home, left for college, and I only go back for holidays."

"Jesus, Layton."

"So there you go, you know it all now. I freeze up when you touch me sometimes, you've seen it, and I know that I have some sense memory of what happened in my head. I've seen counselors, worked through it, and I knew that one day I'd find a man who would make me feel I wanted to fix myself." I turned to look at him again. "I love you, Adler."

I waited for a response—some words to reassure me, or reasons why he couldn't love me. How fucked was I that I couldn't imagine anything between those two extremes?

I think he knew I needed words, but he seemed at a loss for what to say, so he leaned over and kissed me. Then softly, nothing more than a whisper on my lips, he murmured the words I needed to hear.

"I love you too."

Those simple words promised everything; understanding, support, love.

And that was enough.

FOURTEEN

Adler

L ots of people say lots of things about Adler Lockhart, most not good, and rightfully so. I know I can be an ass at times. Words fall out of me before I think about what they are or how they might impact someone. But some-times... every once in a proverbial blue moon... I say the right thing at the right time. Me telling Layton that I loved him in return, yep, that was one of those right thing and right time deals. Mark it down, folks. It probably won't happen too consistently. And not to toot my own horn, but what I did after we had that icy-cold moment of amazing was freaking stellar as well.

I took Layton to his place, because we needed to roll around in the fluffy greatness that was being in love with each other alone. I love Apollo, but knowing he's pitter-pattering around while I'm trying to sex it up with my man isn't conducive to romance. And tonight I was all about the romance. Layton was quiet, vulnerable, and I did my best to keep my inner setter on a short leash. While I wanted to leap on him, knock him down on the ground and lick his face for about eight hours, that wouldn't fly. He needed a calmer lover tonight. He needed his lover to stroke and whisper soft words. He needed his lover to simply adore him. And that was what I planned to do for as long as he would let me.

We'd just gotten our coats off when I moved to his stereo. I popped out the last CD in the player, one of mine, and replaced it with one of his. When I turned, he had one fine dark eyebrow creeping up his forehead.

"I thought we were going to make out a bit," he said. I nodded, then reached behind me to adjust the volume down a bit.

"We are. I'm going to show you just how much I love you." I tugged my shirt over my head and dropped it to the floor.

"So you *can* have sex without that 80s power ballad CD rattling the windows? Good to know." A teasing smile lifted one side of his mouth.

"Well, this won't be the same as something from Cinderella, but I'll manage," I tossed out as "Radioactive" by Imagine Dragons rolled out of the speakers. He'd just burned this CD the other night while I'd been reading some old autobiography about Mario Lemieux. "Come on over here."

He moved to me slowly but not hesitantly, which was great. He trusted me. Nothing had ever made me feel more important than that. Being rich or a reasonably famous athlete didn't even come close. Knowing that this man trusted and loved me? Hell, that made me glow inside. As I reached for him, I hoped he could see the love I felt for him radiating from me. Maybe if he couldn't see it, he could feel it. I gently wrapped him in my arms, nuzzling his long neck as he settled into my embrace.

"You're so perfect here, Layton," I whispered over his jugular.

He wiggled closer, eager to press his erection into my hip bone. A soft moan left my lips. My hands skimmed his ribs, then danced over his lower back, settling on his firm ass. As much as I wanted to jerk him into me or throw him onto the couch, I did neither of those things. I wanted no trace of those fear feelings that crept up over him at times.

His reply was to run his hands over my chest. His fingers roamed over my pectorals. I just held his ass loosely, no pressure, allowing him to touch and gyrate as he wished. His hands went everywhere as we stood there in his living room, swaying ever so gently to Sia's "Bird Set Free" which flowed into my consciousness, the lyrics a perfect representation of this man pressing soft kisses to my jaw as he melted in my arms.

"Let's go to bed," he murmured, with a nip to my neck that made me weak and wanton.

He led and I followed, my fingers between his. His tidy bedroom was familiar now. I'd spent all kinds of time there of late, rolling around with him, getting off with him, whispering under the covers with him. Layton turned and pulled me to him. He unzipped my pants, slid them down my legs, and helped me step out of them. He wiggled my briefs down over my hard-on, then to my ankles, balancing me as I stepped out one foot at a time then peeled off each sock, his gaze flickering over my body, touching everywhere.

"You okay so far?" I asked. He took me in hand. My cock leaped at his touch.

"Let's go to bed," he repeated, his voice as smoky as a wood fire.

He tugged me along to the wide bed by my cock, his eyes now locked with mine. We fell onto the silvery-blue comforter with him still gripping my prick. I threw my arms out to the sides and let Layton do what he wanted to me. I was his, and I wanted him empowered and eager and totally into this moment between us. He slid over me, fully dressed, and lowered his mouth to mine. Then he began teasing in that way that only he could. It was tempting beyond measure. He repeatedly flicked out his tongue along the seam of my mouth until I whimpered. Then he kissed me passionately, his hands fisted on either side of my head, his cock rolling over mine in a steady rhythm that was just this side of torture.

"Sweet shit," I gasped when he broke the kiss and began working my neck with his teeth. Tender little bites that made me squirm and hiss. He nibbled one nipple then the other, sucked a bit of belly skin between his nice white teeth and suckled, then came back to my mouth. He did that several times.

"Layton, God."

"You okay?" he asked between sucking bites along my hip bone. My cock rested by his cheek. All he'd have to do was turn his head to suck my dick into his mouth. My hips flicked upward as I tried to entice him to do just that.

"Are you?" That was paramount.

"Yeah, I'm loving this. I love you." His pewter eyes locked with mine. I fisted the bedding as I fought the need to toss him onto his back and get inside him. That might never happen, and I was cool with it. More than cool with it. Still, the instinctual drive to bury myself deep within the person I loved was always kicking around in my skull unbidden.

"Love you too."

He slithered from the bed and stripped. I watched, my fingers wound in his bedspread, my heart thudding against my ribs, and my cock ready for whatever he wanted from it. When he was nude, he stood at the edge of the bed, looking at me, the head of his prick slick with precum.

"Can you slide around?" He made a circular motion with his finger.

I slid so fast it was a wonder sparks didn't fly from my ass as it zoomed across his comforter. He dropped one knee beside my ear. His dick bounced off my nose. I tried to give it a quick lap, but it bobbed out of tongue-reach.

"Oh shit, Layton, this is… I can't do words about how glorious this is right now," I said as he settled over me, his mouth dropping over my cock as his prick grazed my cheek. "Ah fuck," I groaned as hot and wet surrounded me.

I turned my head and sucked the head of his cock into my mouth. His body trembled as he pulled in a shaky breath around my prick. He sucked roughly, getting me to the edge in no time. I had to get him there too, fast, because this had to end with both of us hitting a climax at the same time. I ran my index finger through the spittle coating his cock, then pressed into his ass, just to the first knuckle.

He mumbled something, but since his mouth was full of my dick, what he said was hard to understand. Didn't matter. I knew he liked what was going on, because he pressed back onto that finger and rotated his hips. A few taps of his prostate, and he was there on the cusp with me. He pulled off when my ass left the bed, and finished me by hand. I grabbed one sweet ass cheek and pulled him downward, choking a bit when he bucked and pumped during his orgasm.

"Ah, ah, oh hell…" Layton gasped as he continued to stroke me, milking every drop before stopping.

I spent all kinds of time cleaning off his cock with my tongue before he tossed a leg over my head and flopped to the bed on his back. I lay there winded for a second, then pushed up and looked at him. His eyes were closed, his chin and chest laced with semen. He looked utterly blissed out.

"This is the best New Year ever."

I scrabbled around on the bed. He cracked an eye open to see what I was doing. "You think so?" I asked before I dropped down beside him and ran a finger through a few dots of spunk drying on his chest.

"I know so."

That made me incredibly happy. "I'm crazy in love with you, Layton."

He threw his arms around my neck and kissed me with wild passion. "You have to be crazy to be in love with me. I'm a fucking train wreck, Ad."

"Good thing we work for the Railers, then. See what I did there? Railers and trains and... sorry. Really sorry, the bad joke filter slipped or something."

He blinked at the stupidity of my comment. Then he laughed, and it was the most glorious thing I'd ever heard. Well, right after the sound of him saying he loved me, of course.

WHEN I WOKE up the next morning, Layton was tight to my back, his arm resting on my hip, one leg between mine. It was so nice I just rested there for a few minutes, enjoying the weight of him pressed to me as well as the smell of sex and man that filled the bedroom. The alarm on my phone went off. Cursing under my breath, I slithered out from under him, found my cell in my pants pocket, and turned the damn thing off.

"Maybe June sometime," Layton mumbled. I snorted, tossed the covers over his tempting body, and jumped into the shower.

I had morning skate in about two hours, and a game tonight. Then we were jetting up to Boston to play Brady Rowe and his big, bad boys. Tennant was all kinds of pumped. After the Boston game, we'd jump to Pittsburgh for the first of a back-to-back that would find us playing in Harrisburg the next night against Pittsburgh again. Knowing I'd be gone for the best part of a week, I wanted to make sure this morning was extra special, to match the extra-specialness of last night.

I decided to cook.

It couldn't be that hard, right? I mean, you just throw eggs into a pan and toss some bread into the toaster. Voila! Breakfast. It wasn't like I was making something fancy like Apollo made all the time. I hustled around, because time was key. I had to get home, grab a suit, and haul it to the barn. Maybe I should bring some clothes over here. I pondered on that as I slapped some butter into a pan that I'd found in the dishwasher. Just a couple of suits and some casual stuff. I was here just about all the time and this running home for clean underwear was a pain in the ass. I'd think on it while on the road.

The butter in the pan sizzled. "Cool," I muttered, then went to my phone for some tunes. I was feeling all kinds of great, so no soft or sad shit. Rick Astley blasted forth and all was good in the world. I danced across the kitchen as Rick pledged never to give his girl up. Dropping four slices into the toaster, I sang along with Rick, because I felt the same way. I'd never make Layton cry, or lie to him, or say goodbye to him.

"The butter's burning," Layton shouted over Rick.

I spun from the toaster. He nodded his rumpled head at the stove. I stopped dancing and grinned.

"You look amazing this morning," I told him.

A shy smile tugged at his lush mouth. Wearing nothing

but some baggy lounge pants that rode low on his lean hips, the man was the picture of disheveled, well-loved sexiness. And fuck me, but that thin line of dark hair leading into his waistband was the most erotic thing I'd ever seen. I needed to lick it.

"Thanks. The butter is still burning."

I threw the frying pan a look. Smoke was curling upward.

"And that's not good?"

Layton rolled those gray eyes theatrically, then pattered to the stove and turned down the flame. Robert Palmer started singing. I wiggled my way to the man at the stove, kissed him on the back of the neck, then slipped my arms around him.

"I'm all kinds of addicted to your love," I purred by his ear as he cracked a few eggs into the brown butter in the pan. Hands on his hips, I moved him back and forth to the steady beat. He laughed again, then began moving on his own. My life could not possibly get any better.

"My mother listens to this type of music," he said while scrambling our eggs.

"You love it and you know it. Just look at your backside moving." I lapped at his shoulder where it joined his neck.

"You're doing that." I removed my hands from his hips and his ass kept moving. "Shit, you've infected me with Rick Astley."

"The love of the 80s is strong in this one," I chuckled beside his ear. He turned in my arms, his eyes light and playful. He kissed me long and deep. I gathered him close as his tongue slipped and curled around mine.

"The love of Adler Lockhart is strong in this one," he whispered when the kiss ended.

"You literally just killed me a thousand times right

there. God, I adore you." I covered his mouth with mine until the smoke alarm went off.

We ate out and held hands. On the table where everyone could see. That was my idea, as was the two plates heaped high with French toast and vaguely burned eggs. Eating was hard. I kept getting lost in pewter eyes and those tender smiles across the table.

"I love you," I told him as he buttered his stack of toast. "I love you and I want to come out."

He laid his knife and fork down beside his plate and pinned me with a look. "Ad, are you sure? That's a huge decision."

"I'm sure. I want to tell the world I love you. I want to take you out and hold your hand and fill you up with French toast."

"You can do that and not make a big public display of things." Our server came back with more coffee. We got our cups topped off without ever looking away from each other.

"Don't you want me to come out? Are you worried about how it will impact you? Is it freaking you out? I won't come out if it's ticking bad boxes for you," I said after he went off to fill other empty mugs.

"Adler, it's not that. I'm fine with whatever you want to do. I want you to be out if *you* want to be out, but I think you might be swept up in the feelings we have for each other." His gaze darted to an older couple passing our booth. The pancake house was hopping. "You do tend to do that."

"I don't," I argued. He gave me a stony look. "Okay, maybe I do let my emotions carry me along at times, but this isn't one of those times."

Ah, there was that smile. It was so pretty. "Tell you

what. Take this week away to think about it. Don't be hasty."

"I don't *ever* do hasty things and I will prove it to you. Don't make that face."

"Adler, your picture is next to the word 'impulsive' in the dictionary."

"No, it is not." Okay, it totally was, but I wasn't backing down on this. "I'll think about it while I'm on the road with the team. When I come back I'll still feel the same way."

"That's fair. Now eat your breakfast." He waved his fork at my food as if the discussion was over. "We have to get you to the arena in thirty minutes or you'll be late for morning skate."

"I'm not impulsive all that much," I mumbled, and sawed at my pile of French toast.

Layton said something under his breath that had the words "setter" and "impetuous" in it. The rest was lost because I opted out of listening. I'd show him. Just you watch. I'd be Mr. Not Impulsive. I could do that for a week.

———

I BURST into Layton's office as soon as we got back from Pittsburgh. His gray eyes shone with pleasure when he looked up and saw me taking up all his office space.

"Hey babe, look at this!" I wrenched off my jacket, unbuttoned my shirt, removed my tie, and tugged my shirt down off my shoulder to show him the tattoo I'd got while in Boston. "It's a Pokémon because I joined the Railers Pokémon group." I wiggled my shoulder to get him to say something and to make Arcanine dance.

"Uh," he said, then laid his pen—the one I'd bought

him—down on his blotter. "Since when do you play Pokémon?"

"Well, I don't yet, but I'm going to. And all the other guys in the group have inkwork and they said if I was part of the group then I needed a tat. Sweet, huh?"

He was fighting back a smile. "So let me get this right. You got this tattoo on a whim because someone said you should, even though you've never played this game in your life?"

I tugged my shirt up to cover the yellow creature sitting high on my left biceps. "Mostly."

"And you still maintain that you're not impulsive at all?"

I shoved my tie into the front pocket of my pants. "When you say it like that, it sounds a little rash."

The laugh broke free. I loved making him happy. If a tattoo did that, I'd be inked from asshole to ears within a year. "I really missed all your spur-of-the-moment Adlerness."

I bumped the door shut with my ass. The sassy smirk never left his mouth. The mouth that badly needed to be kissed. By me.

"You should get one that matches mine. Oh, here's an idea. We both get Arcanine on our arms, then we just parade around town with our biceps out. People see it, do the two and two makes four, and we're out."

"First off, I am not getting a tattoo. You can forget that idea. Secondly, it's late January in Pennsylvania. Your new cat ink would get frostbitten."

"I don't think he's a cat. I'm not sure what he is. A dog, I think." I peeked into my shirt at the tattoo. "He's cute, though. And I'm not Tennant Rowe. I can handle the cold. Can I kiss you here in your office, or is that not professional?"

"I think you and I left professional in the dust."

I leaned on the closed door, scooted down a few inches, and waited. My man rose from his seat behind his desk, slowly made his way around all the furniture, and was finally pressed tight against my chest, his hands raking through my hair.

"You're so ginger."

"You so missed me."

His fingers moved softly over my scalp. "Yeah, I so did."

He kissed me in a way that was so unprofessional but incredibly hot.

FIFTEEN

Layton

I'd begun to dread the messages that I saw when I went into the office, despite the fact that managing that crap was my job. Twitter flared up every hour or so, and some of the comments out there about the Railers were just plain nasty. Nothing I hadn't seen before, but still, I couldn't help but feel like some of what was thrown was directed at me personally. That morning, though, I didn't even have to make it into the damn arena to see the vitriol being thrown about.

I'd handled things like this before, but that was before we added the very real fear that being with Adler would cause everything to go sideways. I'd managed situations before where hate was commonplace, but never where it had touched me in such a visceral, personal way.

And I didn't think I was coping. In fact there was no thinking about it. I knew I wasn't coping. What the Railers were doing here was a million steps forward for equality in pro sports, but on a personal level would the Railers be the ones who had to pay the ultimate sacrifice? Would they survive? Would Jared and Ten make it through this?

Hell. Was Adler going to be hurt?

And why in fuck's name was I feeling so dramatic this morning?

I saw the group standing outside the security gate, some in security uniforms, a couple of players; I recognized Arvy and Stan straight away. There was a commotion, some shoving and pushing, and I pulled over, willing to at least try to do part of my job even if this was a hockey issue.

I jogged over and made some sense of what I was seeing. Stan was holding Arvy back, two of the security guards bickering and forming a brick wall between them and a third security guy.

Arvy was shouting, "He was here. If he says he didn't see anything—"

Stan pulled Arvy a little further back, and I slid between them and the security guys. I immediately looked to Bill, the same guy I saw in uniform every morning, the one whose kids were in college, the same man who always said good morning. He looked gray.

"What's wrong?" I asked, and held up a hand to stop Arvy talking even as he let out a loud curse word. I spun to face him. "Go in," I snapped. "Cameras." I waved behind them, where sometimes we had groups of people waiting for the players, taking photos, and getting autographs. There were only two that morning, some way back, and neither of them seemed to be pointing phones our way.

Arvy subsided and shook off Stan, stalking past security and deliberately hip-checking the new guard at the back, who flinched and moved aside. Stan followed, stopping to talk to the guard in a low voice. What he said, I couldn't hear, but it was enough for the young man to pull himself tall and nod.

Funny how Stan, with the least grip on English in the team, had the best things to say.

"Tell me," I said again.

The two guards in front of me, Bill and one I didn't know, maybe a night guy, looked at each other. Then, with a sigh, Bill moved to one side, and I saw it.

The most unoriginal gay slur of all time. "Fags play here."

I sighed and looked at the third guard, who seemed to be close to losing his shit in a 'falling to the ground crying' kind of way.

"Let's get this removed," I said. "Get a maintenance guy out here."

"On it," Bill said, and went into the small security hut.

I shrugged off my jacket, the biting cold of an early Pennsylvania morning not enough to deter me. I covered over the graffiti and stood there, but I needed something—anything—to hold it in place.

"Here," Adler said in a soft voice, and leaned over me with a roll of hockey tape. He taped the jacket, and we stood back looking at it critically. We could still see the "e" of *here*, but that could be anything. Adler passed me his coat, and I opened my mouth to argue until he raised an eyebrow and it reminded me of what he'd said about the cold. Also, if I made a fuss, then someone could say something, as if they knew that Adler was kissing me, sleeping with me, and that we'd used both our cars just as a cover up. Abruptly, I didn't want that to be a thing when we were standing there in that shitty situation.

"How did this happen?" I asked the new guy, who couldn't quite look me in the eye.

"I didn't see anything," he said, and I stared long enough that he finally looked at me. Then he hung his head. "I'm sorry. I needed the restroom, and Ed was on rounds."

Maintenance was there in minutes and it made me think there was paint on standby for cases like this. Had it happened before Ten had come out?

I closed my eyes briefly as my cell vibrated and I saw Cote's name on the screen. The owner couldn't have heard about this already, could he?"

"Foxx?" he said. "Are you dealing with this?"

I nodded mutely, then realized what I was doing. "Yes, sir," I said. He hung up before asking any questions.

We'd been doing so well, managing the hate, community events to raise the profile of the Railers, and the day before I could have walked into the arena confident that the Railers would make it through this.

Now, this morning, I was shaken.

By the time I reached my office I was a mess of concern, and felt sick when I booted up my PC and waited for the notifications.

Ironically, last night had been quiet on the 'net. There were a couple of new memes about Ten and Jared— nothing I couldn't handle by tweeting an infographic the marketing team had given me about the recent successes on the road. I had a picture putting Ten's stats into perspective against his brothers'. But if I used that, then all I was doing was drawing attention to his 'brothers' teams, and the management of each of them were already a little edgy about certain things going down at the Railers, and how they might be affected before I'd properly begun my work with them.

Like at the game last week when some kid behind the bench had somehow managed to throw a cup of lukewarm coffee at Jared, soaking him when it hit his shoulder.

Which had led to TV time, where the incident had

been played on repeat, and everything circled back to the concept that it was the *gay issue*. How could I even begin to spin the fact that the cameras had caught gay slurs?

And the kid really had been a kid. No more than thirteen, egged on by his mom, of all people.

I scrubbed my eyes and pulled a notepad toward me, making a note of what I needed to do today. First off, I had to get my head around creating an assessment of everything that was happening. When I finished, it felt to me like we were still winning. The community was behind us, the fans for the most part were accepting, only a few people had canceled season tickets since the presser, and the original heavy influx of hate emails had trickled down to a few in among well-thought-out and considered reactions. The tone of the reactions to Ten coming out had changed subtly, particularly when it was Ten who'd put up two goals against Pittsburgh in an emphatic win.

The game tonight was a home game, and I didn't know much about the team we were facing, only that they were rivals in a way that meant the fans were big on chanting at each other and holding up signs, some of them probably designed to put our team on the back foot.

I wrote down some notes about what to say to Coach Benning and went off to find him, locating him in his office with its open door policy and its wall of pictures of players, teams, and a couple with the Stanley Cup, which I knew meant a lot to hockey players. Benning was old guard, and I'd expected that he'd be the most reluctant in this entire process, but he'd been surprisingly affable.

I knocked on the doorjamb. "May I speak to you?"

He gestured me in. "You want to shut the door?"

I didn't think he was asking me—he sounded resigned —and I shut the door and leaned against it.

"Some tweets, posts, they talk about tonight's game,

and I want to reassure you that management takes any and all threats to player safety very seriously." I stopped, because that sounded a lot like management-speak, and I despised that. Also, Coach Benning was shaking his head.

"You take care of security; I'll stop my players from killing anyone if they get all riled up."

That was exactly what I wanted to hear. I needed to know that the players were safe, and that they'd taken my talks to heart. Only Coach would be able to paint it black and white enough for the team to take the words to heart.

Not to rise to the words thrown at them. Not to get angry.

When I left his office, leaving the door open, I deliberately walked the long way back to my tiny office, just to avoid the chance of meeting any players. I wasn't ready to look any of them in the eye and tell them to relax and not to worry.

Because I would be telling them the opposite of what I felt.

When I reached my office, I reported the latest batch of threatening tweets to the authorities, who logged everything because that was all they could do.

Then I shut myself in my office and dealt with the things I could handle; the connection between our team and Boston's and the reaching-out from two Canadian teams. Things I could control.

And I didn't worry about what would happen tonight, or if Ten had a target painted on his back.

But most of all I had to forget Adler and his naive assertion that he was happy to come out to everyone, like it wasn't the hardest thing for a pro athlete to do. He said he trusted me to change people's perceptions, one team at a time. I wished I felt as positive.

. . .

I WATCHED the warmups from the press box, distracted more by watching the crowd than the team. There was a healthy swathe of the opposing team's colors, but I hadn't spotted any posters from them or the home fans when the camera panned the crowd. Everything appeared calm, just two groups of fans, one bigger than the other, there to watch a hockey game.

Tonight was the Railers' night; the battle wasn't easy, but the win, a shutout, was hard fought, and I knew enough about hockey now to get the impression that we'd played well. Apart from some chanting, which was directed more at poor Stan in goal than the rest of the team, the crowd was good-natured.

The opposing team left the ice, and the Railers were head-bumping Stan and offering half hugs. Stan took a little longer to leave the ice, but he had this complicated patting that he did to his net, which Adler had explained was Stan's way of thanking the net for its help. He was last off the ice, winding his way slowly toward the bench, his helmet pushed up on his head. He'd squirted water on his face and was grinning. I saw Ten waiting for him by the tunnel, pulling him into a hug. There were quick movements where they stood, but I was used to seeing Stan and Ten's complicated handshake thing, which involved too much ass-slapping to be completely straight. I was smiling at that even as the press room went deadly quiet. Stan was on the ice, Ten hunched over him, and security was at the tunnel.

I didn't think. I just ran.

I'd never seen so much blood on the ice, but Adler was right by me, still in his uniform, reassuring me that head wounds bled like fuck, and it was likely just a cut.

Ten had tossed a puck up to a kid in the stands by the tunnel, and the kid's dad had thrown it back in temper. Stan, with his goalie reflexes, had moved between the puck and Ten, the puck smashing into him. Stan hit the ice hard.

So much blood, added to the fact that the medics took Stan off the ice on a stretcher.

Security hustled the dad and the crying kid away from the remaining crowd, and the players, who all wanted a piece of whoever had hurt their goalie. Nowhere had I ever seen the "protect the goalie" mentality more than in the locker room of irate skaters. I hovered at the back of the room. What was I going to say? What could I have done? That poor kid, no more than seven or eight, had heard his dad spewing hate and watched the violence right there.

Ten was quiet, Jared sitting next to him, their knees pressed together. Ten was pale and Jared looked ready to kill someone. All I could think was that I'd lost control of the situation. Words weren't going to stop the hate.

What had the team been thinking, hiring me to fix this problem? All I wanted to do was shove everyone back into the closet and hide in there with them where it was safe.

The door opened and Stan ambled in, his face bruised and swollen, stitches over his eye.

"Am okay," he announced, and waved his hands in front of his face. Everyone crowded him. He was leaving to see a specialist, but that wasn't going to stop him celebrating a shutout first.

The worst part wasn't when Ten hugged him, it was when Jared did, thanking him in a broken voice.

. . .

I DIDN'T GO STRAIGHT HOME, DRIVING aimlessly and thinking about what could and couldn't be done right now. I'd spent a couple of hours on damage control, and was proud of the fans who were part of a groundswell of support for Stan, and then Ten and Jared. Most were horrified, and when players on other teams began to retweet calls for upgraded player safety, it appeared that something had come out of Stan covered in blood, taking a puck to the face for Ten.

When I finally arrived home, I knew Adler would be there. He didn't have a key to my place; that was something I'd been working up to, back when I'd had hope that I was doing the right thing. Now? Well, fuck, I wasn't so sure.

Adler pushed himself away from the wall as I unlocked my door, and followed me inside. He hugged me from behind when the door was shut, and for a few seconds I allowed that. He'd mended that part of me that would have pulled away. I trusted him to hold me and not hurt me. But this had to stop.

"I'm done with this," I said, still facing away from him, still in his arms.

His hold tightened momentarily, then he carefully turned me to face him. "Layton?" He sounded puzzled, but there was still the hint of a smile curving his lips.

I swayed toward him, my body betraying my logical thought that Adler shouldn't be there and needed to leave right away. Determined, I stepped back and away, and his hand dropped from where he'd been lightly holding my arm.

"What's wrong?" he asked.

"Our goalie could have been seriously hurt. I let self-doubt in and I misjudged the mood of the crowd."

Adler shook his head. His smile had slipped a little, but

he had that air about him of a man who didn't see the bad side to any of this.

"It was one man," Adler said.

He stepped nearer to me, but I moved back, going into the kitchen so the counter was between us. I wasn't scared of Adler—I was terrified I would back down if he touched me. Adler needed to be safe, at least for a bit longer. Wait until having an out hockey player was the norm, and not something to be held up and examined. I would still do my job, but I wasn't going to be responsible for Adler lowering his barriers. He'd been a professional hockey player for a long time with his secret—why ruin it just to be with me?

I hadn't even decided I was staying here.

This was just a short-term affair.

Sex. Is all.

I told myself that repeatedly until I almost believed the words.

"I need to focus on this," I began lamely. "On making sure I change the narrative for this situation." I was rambling, I knew I was, but Adler was listening and hadn't come any closer. He pushed his hands into his pockets and waited patiently for me to finish.

"I'm not ready for you to be hurt," I finished.

"I'm old enough to decide for myself," Adler said, his tone careful. "And I love you."

I looked at him, right at him, at the man I'd fallen in love with, and knew I needed space to get my head straight. If he came out, people wouldn't understand.

"I love you too," I said. There was no point in lying. "But I won't be responsible for… I have work to do… I need you…" I stopped, because my thoughts were jumbled, messy and wrong.

"No one will hurt me," he said, and I really think he believed it.

"They called me those names, they cursed me, spat on me, made me into something they could fuck, and then they left me naked on a road, Adler."

I knew right there I'd fucked up. I hadn't told him it was more than one boy who'd hurt me, that it was a group of them who'd been drunk, high and filled with hate.

"They," he murmured. "Layton—"

"I just need some quiet to think this all through," I said, desperation in my voice.

And like the very best man in the entire world, the most thoughtful, considerate boyfriend, the kindest of all souls, he nodded, and left, with a quiet, "I love you— remember that."

I tried.

SIXTEEN

Adler

H e thought I'd left. I guess I had in a way. I was no longer in his space or face, but I was in the hall, staring at the door to his place, willing it to open and to reveal Layton calling me back in. Maybe he'd changed his mind and wanted me around again. After thirty minutes and no open door, I had to accept that he wasn't ready for me now... or ever. I hadn't been good enough again.

And that fear and anger and helplessness and regret and pain all started to coalesce in my breast. I wanted to do something for him, but there was nothing I could do. I wanted to go back in time and find the motherfuckers who'd abused my man and beat them into paste. I wanted to punch holes in the walls of this nice corridor, but I couldn't. So I left his building and I drove around Harrisburg until I ran out of gas. Then I walked. Somehow I ended up by the capitol building. It wasn't open yet. I sat down on the west side on the grand stairs leading up the impressive white building. The ice on the steps made my ass cold. I got up after a bit, hands in my pockets, and continued walking.

I ended up by the Susquehanna River. There were big chunks of ice along the banks. My breath fogged in front of me. I felt hollow inside. Hollow and angry. Angry at that stupid, hateful, homophobic fan for refusing to let his son have a puck from a queer player, the press, my parents, and myself. Somehow my love hadn't been enough for Layton. I hadn't been a good enough boyfriend. Probably because I'd been hiding the fact that I *was* his boyfriend. I'd never been good enough…

And so the rage and self-disgust fed off the confusion and fear, and it quadrupled. It was so large come evening that it was all there was of Adler Lockhart. I was a skating ball of chaos who was on the edge. All it would take would be a comment or a nudge. I got both ten minutes into the game with Philadelphia. The nudge was from Gabriel Marsan, a defenseman from Philly known for being one of those players who likes to push. He rarely made the mistake of being way over the line, but if he could instigate and pull a penalty, then he would. He was good at both— pulling penalties and poking a humming hornets' nest with his stick.

The first slash in the corner, I ignored, although the back of my hand would be bruised from the whack. The second and third slashes, I warned him about. He smiled and asked if I needed my mommy to come kiss the boo-boo. Maybe it was the cadence of his heavy French-Canadian accent, or maybe it was his face or his sweater number. Maybe it was the fact that the man I loved had said he needed time away from me. Probably it was the last, because Gabe and I had never had issues before. Usually I laughed at his attempts to lure me into being stupid. Tonight… well, tonight I was lost in the stupid-angry.

We met up behind our net during a little scrum. Our

backup goalie, Jens Hedlund, had deflected the puck into the boards and it had careened behind his crease. Gabe and I arrived at the puck at the same time. The usual shoulder-to-shoulder pushing happened. We were both after the puck. It was all good. He managed to shuttle the puck between my skates where Tennant—who still looked haunted and sick with guilt about his best friend Stan's injury—picked up the rolling puck and headed down to the other end of the ice. Gabe's stick ended up between my legs in what should have been called a trip. I went down and took the big D-man down with me. Luck had me landing on top of him. The officials had followed the puck, or so I thought.

"Get the fuck off me unless you're looking for a kiss, Lockhart," Gabe snarled, then winked. Normally I might even have kissed him on the visor just for the yuks. Tonight I took that wink to mean something that, upon reflection with a clear and happy heart, it was not. Gabe's helmet somehow ended up in my hands, and I proceeded to bounce his melon off the ice a few times. He got his stick up and cracked me on the chin with it. Blood began to flow. Whistles blew. Men in black and white grabbed at me and pulled me off Gabe, who was stunned by the violence. Sure, that's hockey, but he and I had history, and we'd joked with each other for years now. I lunged at him, then was escorted from the ice. A trainer joined me, shoving a towel at my chin to catch the blood leaking out of me.

I heard the announcer calling my penalties as I stormed under the now covered tunnel to the home locker room. Nice. An instigator and a game misconduct. That was it for me this game. Most of what followed, I didn't mentally register, aside from the fact that we'd lost the game. I got fourteen stitches in my chin, then got my ass peeled like a Cortland apple by Coach Benning. It was well deserved. The team was staggered from the loss of Stan coupled with the hate directed at Ten and Jared, and now I'd just added more stress to the situation. And the worst thing about the whole stupid fray was that now I'd vented some of that toxic self-loathing, I knew my actions would impact the one person I was trying my best not to hurt.

Layton.

It would be him pressured into making me look like less of an asshole than I was. I stripped off my gear and threw it into my cubicle, then showered alone. I scrubbed my face so violently that I tore out six stitches and had to have them resewn. This time I opted out of a shot to deaden the area. Maybe the pain would straighten me the fuck out. By the time I was done being sewn up, the other players were off the ice and heading home. I caught sight of Tennant as I exited the team doctor's office. He was having a deep conversation with someone on his phone. His gaze met mine as I neared. He held up a finger, so I stopped in front of him.

"No, Brady, I'm handling it." Ten rolled his eyes, but there was little humor in them. None of us were feeling particularly chipper. "Look, I have to go. Yep, I'll tell Mads you said to hang in there. Uh-huh. Later."

He shoved his phone into the front pocket of his dress slacks. He was ready to exit the arena as well.

"Big brother worried?" I asked.

"It's his perpetual state." Tennant sighed. "Walk with me. I want to talk to you."

I fell in beside him as we began wending our way through corridors, past offices and skate-sharpening rooms, until we stepped into the now-empty press room. Tennant shoved the door shut, then gave the area a long look, his expression pensive.

"What's up?"

"You know, I hate this room at times." He scowled at the chairs that held the press corps. "I mean, it's not the media that's the reason for all of this hate. It's really not," he added, then glanced at me for confirmation. I nodded. "It's people. People hate. Governments hate. Religions hate. And the press, they just pick up the vibes and report them."

"Do you regret coming out?" That question had been on my mind ever since the presser that Layton had so magnificently orchestrated. Fuck, but I missed him. It was like I'd lost a limb or an organ. Well, my heart had shattered and blown away like dust, so I guess I had...

"No, not for a second." He was adamant, but then the determination slipped from his face a bit. "Let me amend that. I do *not* regret the decision Mads and I made to come out. I do regret that our being in a relationship has brought pain and injury to one of my best friends. I just... I can't stop feeling the weight of that moment. That Stan is now hurt because of me. That's giving me some trouble."

"Ten, it wasn't you who hurt Stan, it was hate. Blind, stupid, black-hearted hatred that knocked our goalie out." I bent to the side to catch his eye.

He bobbed his head in that way guys do when they want you to think they agree but they *really* don't. "Thanks for that. Mads tells me the same thing on a fucking hourly basis, but the guilt is still there, like an anchor sitting on my chest." He inhaled, then let the breath out slowly. "You thinking of coming out?"

My mouth and brain skipped out of sync. The first real smile in days appeared on Tennant Rowe's face.

"I— What?" I stammered.

"Ad, seriously, it's pretty obvious to anyone with eyes in their head. The way you look at Layton Foxx and the way he responds to you entering a room? It's evident you two have something powerful going on." He leaned against the wall by the double doors, his sharp green eyes riveted on me.

"I… Uh, I'm not sure where we are, so it's not like I'm ready to go talking about it, you know?" Wow. I'd just come out to Tennant. And it felt… okay.

"Oh yeah, I know," he said with an understanding nod. "It's like being paint in a can. You're just this one bland color, right? Like dull old white. And then someone opens the lid and adds this beautiful new color. Maybe it's aqua or violet or magenta. And then you both get put into a machine that shakes and stirs the living shit out of you. You want to puke and laugh and cry, but you're spinning too madly to even know what emotion to feel. Then the whirling slows and you and he are this new, totally amazing color. A combination of colors that's beautiful and makes your eyes water."

"That was poetic," I murmured. Ten's nose wrinkled in embarrassment. "It feels like Layton and I are in the whirling and vomiting part of things now." I shoved my hands under my armpits. "But after all the gyratory shit, it gets better, right?"

The door opened. Coach Madsen peeked around it. The look on his face when he spied Tennant answered my question better than any words could have. These two men loved each other so strongly it made me feel weepy. I wanted that with Layton.

"Hey, here you are." Coach looked at Ten, then at me. "Adler, you going to be able to sit down anytime soon?"

"Not for a few days," I replied, both of us referring to the ass-chewing I'd gotten from the head coach.

"Hopefully the league will go light on you." He clapped my shoulder. "Ten, you ready to go home?"

"Yeah, give us a sec, okay?" Ten smiled at Mads. You could feel the adoration for Jared flowing from Tennant.

"Sure." Coach Madsen gave his boyfriend a curious look but backed out of the room, leaving us to it.

"Okay, so here's the thing I wanted to talk to you about. I got your back, okay? You and me, we fit. Our line is gelling. This team has potential. All our personal shit aside, you belong on this team, and I consider you a Railers player now. I mean, you have Arcanine on your freaking arm now. You're one of us."

"Thanks, that means a lot." I offered him my hand. He bumped it aside and grabbed me for a fast, hard hug.

"It's worth it, Adler," he reassured me, then jogged off to find Coach Madsen and go home. Together. As a couple.

Knowing I had to apologize for being a fuckup, I left the arena, slid behind the wheel of my BMW, and ended up back where this whole miserable slide into the slurry pond had begun. At Layton's place. My phone started ringing. It was Apollo. I let it go to voicemail. There was no way I could handle him right now. He'd be all in my face demanding to know what moronic madness had overtaken my brain. I turned off the engine and sat in my car until I could see my breath. Layton's light was still on. He was probably working his social media magic to pull my sorry ass out of the fire. Like he needed that.

"I suck so much," I sighed, the words a fat puff of steam that settled on the windshield and turned to more ice.

Without words to say, I made my way to his door. My chin hurt, my heart ached, and I just wanted to hold him because he was suffering too. I knocked. I could hear him walking to the door. There was a pause—him looking through the peephole, more than likely.

"If you don't want to talk to me now, I get it. I just…" I put my hand on his doorknob and stroked it in lieu of him. My gaze dropped to my fingers. "I just wanted to let you know that I'm sorry, babe. For everything bad that has ever happened to you. If I could, I'd carry that burden for you. I'd suck all the pain and fear out of your soul and carry it in mine."

The knob was cool at first, smooth too, but as I caressed it the metal began to warm to my touch. I doubted the man on the other side of the door ever would again. The pain of thinking that nearly dropped me to my knees.

"I know I've added more shit to the mess you're dealing with." I blew out a long breath, my fingertips still resting on his doorknob. "I'm sorry for that too, Layton. The only thing I ever wanted to do was make you happy, because your smile? Wow. It's all the beauty of the world wrapped up into one grin to me."

The door opened. My fingers fell to my side and my gaze slowly climbed up over him. He was so fucking handsome, and I was so close to losing him. His gray eyes moved over my face and settled on the ugly black stitches in my chin.

"Why did you do that?" The question was soft and heartfelt.

I thought on that for a minute as I stared into pewter eyes that would be with me forever even though he probably wouldn't be.

"I wanted to bleed for you. I wanted to feel the pain that you did. I wanted to hurt someone for the crime committed against you. Gabe was the unlucky person."

He remained silent. I took that as my sign to leave.

"Okay, well, I just wanted to see you one more time. To

tell you I love you." I took a step backward and went to turn.

"Don't go."

"Yeah?" I couldn't bring myself to look at him yet, in case I'd misheard.

"Yeah."

I stood in the hallway, staring at a small stain on the carpet, scared to move even though my heart was flinging itself against my ribs like a newly caged bird.

"Adler, come in," Layton said in a firm voice.

I glanced up. He looked like he might just still love me, even though I'd done nothing to deserve any kind of—

"Stop whatever self-hating 'I'm not good enough for you' monolog is running in your head now."

"It's the truth." His eyes were warm, right? Was that warmth I saw in his eyes? "I love you so much." That just fell out of me. It was the softness in his gaze that made me say stupid things.

"No, it's not. You deserve to be loved, and I love you too. Now get in out of the hallway before the neighbors hear us pledging our troth." Oh my God, he smiled a little.

I smiled a lot. "I don't care if they hear me, Layton. Hand to *all* the gods above, I do not care. I want the world to know."

"I can really only douse so many fires at once, Ad. I'm not Smokey Bear." He waved a hand to encourage me inside. I slid into his space but not into his face. He closed the door.

"Would it be okay if I held you for, like, one second?" I prayed he'd say yes.

"I'd like that a lot. I can't seem to focus without you close by."

I opened my arms and let him step into my embrace. *Nothing* would ever match how good he felt in my arms.

The tears just broke loose. I dropped my chin to his shoulder, hissed at the pain, but kept my face hidden. He needed me to be strong, not the other way around.

Layton pressed his hand to the back of my neck. "You can cry if you need to," he whispered, and that blasted all the bricks in the dam to bits.

This was not how it was supposed to be. I was the hockey player. It was my job to hold Layton and give him succor.

"Oh, Ad, it's going to be okay." His hand rubbed small circles between my shoulder blades while the other massaged the nape of my neck. He pressed a kiss to the side of my head as I sniffled and coughed, my fingers tight to his sides.

"I want to be paint with you."

"Oh…kay. I want to be paint with you too?"

A raspy, coughing laugh rolled out of me. "Cool. We're going to make one truly vibrant and unique color, Layton." I clasped him tighter, then spun him around a few dozen times to make sure we were well mixed.

SEVENTEEN

Layton

I had no idea what I was doing.

All the things inside me that told me to back away from Adler had melted away as soon as he'd knocked on my door. Watching him get in that fight, I'd known it was partly my fault. I'd messed with his head, and I was sorry for it—sorrier than he would ever know. To have him there in my arms, clearly emotional, was a moment that would define this thing we had going on between us.

"I called my family," I said, because I needed him to know what I'd done when he'd left; it was vital he understood my fear. He didn't lift his head from my shoulder, but he mumbled something that sounded like a soft "Yeah?"

"I wanted to tell them that I felt like shit when I was at home, that it wasn't their fault, but that we all needed to get over what happened to me and they needed to stop worrying, and I needed to stop avoiding them. It went well for the most part, but after four separate phone calls in which I had to explain myself each time, I was done. So it's up to Zach to tell anyone left."

I felt his shoulders shake and I thought he was getting

emotional again, but he lifted his face this time, and even though his eyes were bright he was smiling.

"Poor Zach," he said.

"He can handle it; he's a big boy."

"Stan gave me a message for you."

"Was it something to do with my eating habits?"

"I only made out half of it, given that I was staring at the stitches he had in his forehead."

I heard the words, but I didn't immediately stiffen and feel bad for Stan. Adler was right—I had no real control over another man's hate. Still, guilt did curl in my stomach, and I had to breathe through the tightness in my chest.

And Adler gave me time to do that.

"So what did he say?" I asked eventually.

"Blah blah, ov, dah, blah, coffee, blah, Snickers."

I smiled at that.

But Adler hadn't finished. "Anatoly confided in me that Stan's little sister had an eating disorder. He didn't go into details, though."

"Oh." That made sense. I could see why Stan was sensitive, given that he was also a professional athlete. If anything, Stan's worry had made me feel a little more conscious of the whole coffee addiction I had going. I made a mental note to research eating disorders and talk to Stan about it. I'd come across research last week about athletes and the amount of food they needed to consume and how strict that could be. I wanted to know everything about the team and what affected them.

"I like Stan," I said.

"I was jealous of Stan," Adler admitted. He cradled my face in his hands and pressed a kiss to my lips.

"You've nothing to be jealous about."

Adler deepened the kiss, and I was pretty helpless against him, holding tight to his biceps as he bent me back a little. I wanted to get my hands into his thick hair, but he was still cradling my face, and anyway we had all the time in the world.

He released his hold a little, and without words he took my hand in his and tugged me a little toward my small bedroom. I let him lead me, and silently we removed clothes, each kissing every tiny part of skin we revealed, tumbling back onto the bed in a twist of limbs. Somehow he was blanketing me, and I felt a soft press of fear, but he knew.

Somehow he knew. He understood.

He moved so I was lying over him, and then he cradled my face again, and kissed me again, and I just melted. I wanted him so much, the insistent tug of need had me writhing against him, and he pressed up against me until the rhythm was too much and I slipped to one side.

"What if I'm never ready?" I whispered against his skin. "What if you can never be inside me...?" I couldn't get past the block in my head.

"What if that doesn't matter?" he replied. "To me or to you. And what if what we do have is absolutely perfect and right?"

Oh god, this rough, sexy, loudmouthed hockey player was playing with my emotions, and I loved him even more.

"You said you liked to—"

"No more talking, Foxxzee," he said, drawling out my stupid hockey surname and rolling again so he was half on me and half off. That way I could move, and it quelled the insistent tug of panic that could take me from the moment.

He was so gentle, this big man, his hands tracing patterns on my skin, and I closed my eyes and reveled in the tenderness of this slow love he was bestowing on me.

I carded my hands through his hair, tugging him closer,

abruptly needing more of his weight on me, and I kissed him as he moved, and groaned into the kiss.

"Not saying you couldn't do things to me," he murmured softly, and kissed me again. "Anything you wanted. Anything that felt right."

The kiss deepened again, and I didn't release my hands, twisting a little more so I could get closer, under him, our cocks hard against each other. I wanted my mouth on him, I wanted to press slicked fingers into him, I wanted him to come so hard he couldn't breathe, but that would have to wait, because right now I was chasing this soft orgasm that was just out of my reach.

"I love you," he said, then repeated it as he pushed himself up on his elbows. I chased the kiss, but he smiled down at me and rolled his hips.

Game over. I was coming so hard that it was me who couldn't breathe, and when he kissed me, rutting against me into the slickness of my cum, my heart expanded with love for him and I was lost.

"I love you, I love you," I repeated over and over as he kissed me and lost himself beautifully to an orgasm. I clutched his shoulders, his biceps, willing him over the edge, and his muscles flexed under my touch.

This man was all mine. And I was never letting him go.

"I CAN'T CHANGE everyone's minds," I whispered into the darkness. We'd ordered pizza, eaten our fill, and crawled back into bed, wrapped around each other, face to face and holding tight.

"What do you mean?"

"I decided today, whatever I do, even when it's the best work I've ever done, it will never be enough."

"You can't give up," Adler said, with steel in his words. He thought I meant I was giving up? That was far from the truth.

"No, you don't understand. I wouldn't give up. I'm not, I can't. I mean, that man with his kid, the one who threw the puck, maybe one day he'll wake up and he'll see the world like we do, right? It could be when his child says he's gay, it could be when his favorite team has a gay player, it could be when he sees an episode of a soap opera and it makes him think. However it happens, one day he'll see. Maybe. But all I can do now is control the narrative. It's all I tell myself. I can help people see, and make sure what they see is right."

"That's why I love you," Adler said. "Because you don't stop, you don't give up, and you see the good in people despite..."

"Despite what happened to me, you mean."

"Yeah." He shifted a little, and I knew he was uncomfortable with this subject, so I stayed quiet. "Does it make you feel... Am I wrong to..."

"Spit it out," I encouraged, with a smile he wouldn't be able to see but could maybe hear in the tone of my voice.

"I want you to know that you can talk about it with me —what happened to you. I may not be in touch with my emotions, but that's because I don't come from a family that nurtures feelings, and I know that."

"Bullshit," I said, without heat. "You have all the feelings, all the time. You look out for your team, you respect others, you laugh, you want desperately to be friends with people—that has to be as far removed from not being in touch with your emotions as it's possible to get."

"You think?"

"I know. So, we've done me," I began, and realized

that gave Evil Adler, as I'd taken to calling his immature side, a chance to come out.

"Twice," he said with a soft laugh, before kissing me hard.

"I meant we've talked about me. What about you? When do I get to meet your family?"

Silence. I could imagine Adler's brain churning that over. I expected him to either ignore the question, amble away from it in an entirely different direction, or make a joke.

When he did none of those and remained silent, I felt a tiny push of concern inside me, and then he spoke.

"They're not like real parents," he said. "Not like you have, with all their fussing and loving and being up in your business and worrying about you and knowing things about you that you'd rather they didn't." He stopped and moved onto his back, pulling me with him and holding me closer. "But, yeah, I want you to meet them. You need to, I guess, if we're doing this thing right."

I knew he didn't have any siblings, had the impression that his parents had been the sort of hands-off parents that most teenagers would have loved.

"They didn't like you playing hockey?"

He huffed a laugh, and it wasn't a nice sound. Instead it was filled with derision, and I wasn't sure if it was aimed at his parents or himself.

"Cole and Karrie Anne from Brampton, Maine," he said. "Where do I start? They didn't like me being born, let alone being a hockey player. The only thing they really had an issue with was with me being gay, but god knows why they did, because they have… let's say a very open marriage."

"You don't call them Mom and Dad," I said. I'd noticed it before.

"They're not like parents. I wasn't the son they wanted."

"You're a good man, Adler—"

"Okay," he interrupted. "I'll take you to meet them if you'll just stop with the nice stuff." He didn't sound angry, and the kiss was gentle. "I'd like you to meet Apollo's parents, though—they're pretty cool, and they were around a lot for me. And to blatantly change the subject, we need to talk about me coming out."

I tensed—I couldn't help myself. Somehow I'd lulled myself into a love that I could keep right here at home, but that wasn't possible, was it? If I wanted to be myself, I had to be *myself.* That made some sense to me, even though I couldn't find the words to vocalize it.

"I want to tell the team," he said. "Ten already knows. We don't have to make a big thing, but I'd like to feel easier with the team. No big announcements or anything, not for a while, so you can control your narrative or whatever it is you call it."

"You've been taking notes."

"Always. I want to share and help with what Ten is having to handle, along with Jared. Does that make your job harder?"

I smiled into another kiss.

"Having someone who loves me, and whom I love, makes my life easier," I reassured him, and ignored the concern that scratched at the edge of the words. Nothing worth anything was ever easy.

"So we're doing this, then," he said.

"Yeah. I love you."

"Love you too," he murmured, and buried his face in my neck, sighing against my skin. "So much."

Epilogue

ADLER

J*une*

IT WAS STUPID TO CHECK. I knew that. Yet...

"Are you still not ready?" Layton padded up behind me.

I gave him a quick glance over my shoulder. The shoulder that still didn't have a shirt covering it. He held up a pale blue sweater and shook it. Then his gray eyes flickered to the phone in my hand. He lowered the sweater he'd bought me as concern darkened his incredible eyes.

"Maybe they're just out of service somewhere."

"Yeah, maybe not." I shoved my phone into the back pocket of my jeans, then took the sweater from Layton. "It's okay. I mean, it's only my birthday. Why should they stop being Cole and Karrie Anne for ten *fucking* minutes and wish their only son—" I pulled in a calming breath while tugging the sweater over my fat head. "Forget it. We can't make people be what we want them to be, right? We can only control our own narrative."

"That's right." He gave me a wan smile, then handed me my wallet and car keys. I crammed them into a front pocket. "You really do listen when I talk."

"Always, Foxy Man."

I leaned over to steal a fast kiss. His lips were soft, warm, and just too damn tempting. Knowing where one innocent kiss could lead, Layton slipped away before I could get my hands on him.

"The show starts in thirty minutes," he reminded me.

"A night at the arena. Yay."

His scathing look was top notch. "It's not like you're out on the ice." It was a special final show featuring several Olympic figure skaters at the ice that was being melted tomorrow and removed for the summer break. "It's the perfect gift for the man who skates for a living."

"Layton, they wear toe picks."

I pushed my arm into the sleeve of my lightweight dark grey jacket. I'd bought it because when I wore it I was reminded of Layton's eyes. Not that I needed a coat to trigger any kind of memory of the man. He was with me everywhere I went. Buried deep in my heart, calming my brain and making me feel still. That's a rare feeling for me. Only Layton Foxx has ever been able to do that. And make me come so hard with just a whispered word that I nearly black out from sheer pleasure.

"Yes, they wear toe picks." He sighed dramatically. I'd explained the sort-of-friendly rivalry between hockey players and figure skaters. How we chirped each other about who was tougher, better skaters, and which ice sport was harder. "And bright costumes."

I followed him out the front door of his place and waited as he locked things up. I was there pretty much

24/7 now, which gave Apollo all kinds of privacy. I wished he could find someone as amazing as Layton to love.

Since Layton had gone to great trouble to get tickets to the show, I stopped whining about it being a busman's holiday, toe picks, and Trent Hanson, the big star of the ice extravaganza that had rolled into Harrisburg for a one-night-only show.

We hustled to my car parked next to his, a soft summer breeze ruffling his hair.

"Hey," I called, and tossed him my keys. His eyes flared. "You drive."

"Wow, this really must be love." He grinned, grabbed a hard kiss, then got behind the wheel of the Beemer.

"Must be," I said after sliding into the passenger seat. He gave me a sly look, then cued up one of his CDs. "Okay, I'm not sure I love you *that* much," I groaned when "Young and Beautiful" by Lana Del Rey drifted from the speakers.

"Yes you do."

"Yeah, I do."

He eased us out of the parking lot and out into light traffic. We talked about nothing and everything. His cell chirruped about halfway to the arena. He pulled over to the curb to see who was calling. I could tell it wasn't a cheery call by the way the skin on his forehead furrowed.

"Let me take this," he said. I turned the stereo down and leaned back into the seat, watching people walking by enjoying the early summer sun. I caught sight of one woman in a Railers' jersey with Stan's number on the back. Even though the team hadn't made it past the second round of the Stanley Cup finals we had done this city proud, and our following was growing.

Every journalist said one thing; next year we could go further.

"No, Dieter, just let me continue working on the problem. I know. We're going to handle it, but it has to be done properly. Yep. No. I didn't forget. It's okay, I know you're worried. Okay I'll... No, just... Right. That's probably for the best. Good, okay, we'll talk tomorrow."

He ended the call, closed his eyes, and searched for some Zen while I waited.

"Can't talk about it yet?" I asked.

He shook his head. "It's confidential." He opened his eyes and looked at me. "You know I'd tell you if I could."

"It's cool. He's entitled to his privacy. I mean, look how long we kept us a secret."

"This one is complicated."

"You'll get it worked out. You're the best at what you do."

A snort bubbled out of him. "Leaping from one potential social media nightmare to another, you mean?"

"We do keep you busy, huh?" I thought of all the stuff he'd handled since his first day as the Railers social media guru. Tennant and Jared had been huge. Then there had been me, with my mouth that didn't connect with my brain. And now, it seemed, Dieter had something brewing that required Layton's touch.

"You coming out to the team was much easier than Tennant and Jared's coming out to the world." He hit the turn signal, then eased back into traffic. "You still okay with it just being the team and those close to us who know?"

"Yeah, I'm good. The shit with Ten and Jared still hasn't settled. I see the signs at the games and listen to the bigots on TV. I know that's still keeping you and your team dousing blazes."

"And then some," he chuckled. I patted his thigh just to feel his firm flesh twitch under my hand. His gaze touched mine for a second. "The time will come for us to go wide. I want you to be happy."

"There is no possible way I could be any happier than I am right now." He wheeled us into the parking lot of the East River Arena.

"I'm sure there must be something that would make you a little happier." We slipped around back and grabbed a slot right by the players' entrance. Being a Railer had its advantages.

The car had no sooner stopped than someone was hammering on the window beside me. I glared through the glass at Apollo. Wait. Apollo? I put the window down.

"Where have you been? We've been out here for like twenty minutes and I need the bathroom!" My best friend snapped.

"What are you doing here?" I asked. Layton put my window up, turned off the engine and got out. Apollo was dancing and rubbing his biceps when I got out of the car. "I repeat, what are you doing here?"

"Mr. Foxx—Layton, sorry." He gave my man a meek smile. Old habits are hard to break. He'd grown up calling everyone who wasn't in my family's employ Mister, Missus, or Miss, so his formality with Layton was understandable. "Layton wanted your family to be here for your birthday present."

I turned to look at Layton standing beside me. He looked smug. That worried me a bit.

"Adler, would you come tell this man we know you?!" The sound of Mrs. Vasquez giving me the business bounced off the sides of the arena. I gaped at the sight of Apollo's parents up by the players' entrance door. Short Mrs. V with her hands on her hips, and tall Mr. V standing next to her all quiet and thoughtful looking. They looked great. "I told him the story about when you were six and ate twenty-five boxes of raisins and pooped like a goose for three days, but he says we need ID."

The security man gave me a wave and an apologetic look.

I swung my attention to the man on my left.

"Everyone should have their family with them on special days," Layton said softly.

And by all that was holy, he was right. This small group here… this was my *real* family, my *true* family. Apollo and his parents, Layton and his monstrously huge and over-protective kin, and the Railers. Sure, Cole and Karrie Anne had given me their DNA, but nothing else other than money. And money is a poor substitute for affection.

"I swear I love you more than life, Layton," I choked out, then pulled him into my arms.

He melted into me, his arms moving around my waist as if they were made to be there. "I'm pretty fond of you too."

My mouth dropped over his. The kiss held all kinds of promise.

"Let's get your family inside and Apollo to a bathroom."

I slid my fingers into his. We walked into the East River Arena hand in hand, with my family chattering away around us, my arm draped around Apollo.

Best birthday ever. Even with the raisin story coming to light.

THE END

Next for the Railers

Deep Edge (Harrisburg Railers Hockey #3)

One man's passion, another man's lies. Can love fix even the darkest of hearts?

Trent Hanson is a figure skating phenom adored by millions around the world. His whole life has been dedicated to the sport he loves even when the sport - and his own family - have turned against him. From the playground to the Olympics to his parent's living room, Trent has fought against bullies and homophobes to be the out and proud gay man he is. But the constant fighting has left Trent tired, lonely, and skittish.

All those fears will have to be shelved though when he's hired to spend the summer working with the Harrisburg Railers ice hockey team. Who would have guessed that the man fate has decided to pair him off with is Dieter Lehmann, all-around sex god and a man who seems to have everything to prove and doesn't care who he hurts to get what he wants.

Dieter has spent too many years languishing in the

minors, and a secret addiction to prescription painkillers means his career is in a downward spiral. His ex is blackmailing him, and he's close to walking away from it all. But when he's called up in the run for the Stanley Cup to cover injuries he has a taste of what it's like playing in the NHL, and he realizes that a place on the Railers' roster is what he wants more than anything.

More than listening to his heart, and even more than caring for the infuriating figure skater who gets under his skin. When he crosses the line to get what he wants, he knows he has lost his way. He has to change, but is it too late for both his career and any chance he might have at love?

Hockey Series' from RJ Scott & V.L. Locey

Harrisburg Railers

Owatonna U Hockey

Arizona Raptors

Boston Rebels

LA Storm

Chesterford Coyotes - Young Adult

Free Reads

Please note - in all of these free stories, there will be some spoilers for the main series books.

Railers Short Stories

Volume 1 | Volume 2

LA Storm

Sparkle

The Colts - AHL Short Stories

Pucks & Percentages

Breakaway

Making the Save

Standalone

Waiting for Christmas

Harrisburg Railers

When hockey wunderkind Tennant Rowe meets his new coach, he knows he's in trouble. Jared Madsen is nine years older than Tennant, impossibly attractive, and — worst of all — his brother's off-limits best friend. Is their chemistry worth the risk?

Changing Lines (Railers 1)

Can Tennant show Jared that age is just a number, and that love is all that matters?

The Rowe Brothers are famous hockey hotshots, but as the youngest of the trio, Tennant has always had to play against his brothers' reputations. To get out of their shadows, and against their advice, he accepts a trade to the Harrisburg Railers, where he runs into Jared Madsen. Mads is an old family friend and his

brother's one-time teammate. Mads is Tennant's new coach. And
Mads is the sexiest thing he's ever laid eyes on.

Jared Madsen's hockey career was cut short by a fault in his heart,
but coaching keeps him close to the game. When Ten is traded to
the team, his carefully organized world is thrown into chaos. Nine
years his junior and his best friend's brother, he knows Ten is
strictly off-limits, but as soon as he sees Ten's moves, on and off
the ice, he knows that his heart could get him into trouble again.

Changing Lines

Harrisburg Railers (Hockey Romance)

1. Changing Lines
2. First Season
3. Deep Edge
4. Poke Check
5. Last Defense
6. Goal Line
7. Neutral Zone
8. Hat Trick
9. Save The Date
10. Baby Makes Three
11. Rivals
12. Perfect Gifts
13. Family First

---

*Railers Volume 1 | Railers Volume 2 | Railers Volume 3 | Railers
Volume 4*

Meet the men of Owatonna University's hockey team

Ryker (Owatonna U, 1)

Ryker

Ryker is hockey royalty, Jacob is a poor country boy. Can two vastly different people find common ground and become the men they want to be?

Ryker comes from a long line of championship-winning hockey players. Playing college hockey to develop his game is his only focus, and nothing will stand in the way of him working to become the best player. He has no room for relationships, people who point out his flaws, or anyone who calls him on his dreams. He certainly has no place for love, and meeting Jacob is nothing but a useful distraction on the side. After all trying to get his Owatonna Eagles teammate into bed is less work and more play. When tragedy rocks his family, his charmed life crumbles, and the only person he can turn to is the same one who claims to hate him.

Jacob Benson has only known hard work and stifling conservative values his whole life. Born and raised in the small rural community of Eden Crossing, Minnesota, he's the only son of a hard-working but struggling dairy farming family. Jacob is using his skills in hockey to finance his way to an agricultural science degree. These four years at Owatonna U. will probably be the only time he has to enjoy life, gain acceptance about his sexuality, and live openly before his inevitable return to the farm. Running into a pretty rich boy like Ryker Madsen is putting a damper on his enjoyment of life away from home. Ryker's flip, conceited, carefree attitude grates on Jacob's every nerve. So why, if Ryker is everything he dislikes, does he want nothing more than to explore the sinful dreams that his annoying teammate stars in every night?

Ryker

Owatonna U Hockey (Hockey Romance)

Coast to Coast (Arizona Raptors 1)

Coast To Coast

When opposites attract, this bottom-of-the-league team will never be the same again.

A stipulation in his father's will forces Mark back into the arms of a family that disowned him and leaves him one-third owner of a hockey team facing financial ruin. He doesn't even watch hockey, let alone like it, and wants nothing more than to head back to New York. Then there's the new coach, a stubborn, opinionated, irritating man with superiority issues and questionable music taste. Butting heads with Rowen becomes the new normal, but it comes with passionate debate and an all-consuming lust.

Challenged to rebuild one of the worst teams in the league into a future cup contender, Rowen can't pass up the opportunity. Never in his twenty years of hockey has he ever seen a team managed so badly or coached players overflowing with resentment and bigotry. Yet there's something about this team and this city that compels him to roll up his sleeves and start dismantling. If only Mark, one of three siblings who now own the Raptors, wasn't so damned rock-headed yet so damned appealing his job might be easier. It doesn't look like either is willing to give in, but one night in a dark, desert hotel changes everything.

Coast To Coast

Arizona Raptors (Hockey Romance)

1. Coast To Coast
2. Across the Pond
3. Shadow and Light
4. Sugar and Ice
5. School and Rock

Boston Rebels

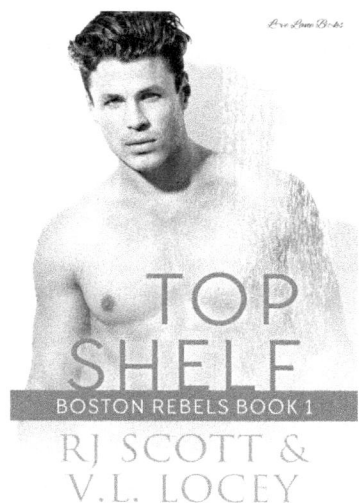

Top Shelf (Boston Rebels 1)

Acting on the attraction to his best friend's brother has always been off the table for Xander until a passionate hookup with Mason at a beach resort begins a love affair that burns long after summer ends.

Mason specializes in assisting same-sex couples on their journey to becoming parents and fighting every rule that blocks his way in the stuck-in-the-past agency that hired him. Living in his brother's pool house is rent-free, and every cent he earns he saves for his dream—that one day he'd have his own company helping others. The downside is that he has to see his annoying brother every day, the upside is that his brother's teammates from the Boston Rebels make regular visits. The eye candy that passes Mason's window is almost enough to make him consider dating a hockey player, but not just any player though. Ever since Xander —his brother's childhood friend—came out as gay at a press conference, Mason's puppy love has turned into a burning attraction he can no longer ignore.

Hockey has been one of Xander's main focuses since he was old enough to balance on skates. Well, hockey and Mason Kingsley, but Mason was always unattainable. Now that he's about to see thirty candles on his birthday cake and is no longer hiding the fact he's gay, he's ready to find a soul mate to make his life complete. A summer vacation is just what he needs to have time to think, but when the Boston Rebels arriving in paradise with Mason in tow, thinking is the last thing he needs. One torrid night under a balmy moon and rules about not messing with his best friend's brother vanish on a warm, tropical breeze.

Summer romances don't generally last past Labor Day, but with the new season about to begin Xander and Mason are going to have to face the world and decide if their love is real enough to withstand everything.

Boston Rebels

Lost In Boston (Free Prequel Novella)

1. Top Shelf
2. Back Check
3. Snowed
4. Royal Lines
5. Blade
6. Rental

LA Storm

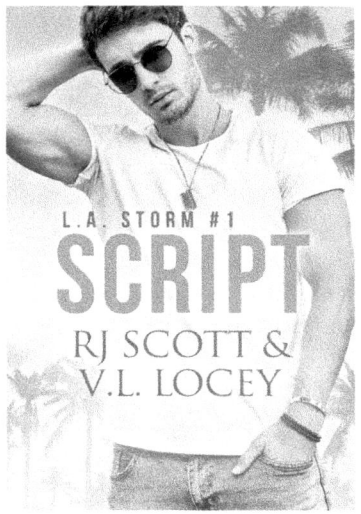

Script (LA Storm, 1)

Script

Hollywood A-lister Finn might be Canadian, but he needs Cameron to show him how to hockey.

Actor Finn Kerrigan is at a crossroads. After growing up a soap star, then starring in a hugely successful trilogy of action movies, he's finally given the chance to read a heartfelt and passionate script that could change his life forever. The role would be enough for people to see him as a serious actor, and maybe even win him an award or two (and no, a golden raspberry award for his action movies doesn't count). Once established as a serious actor he's sure he can come out of the closet and finally live his truth. When he lies to get the part of a hockey player on a struggling team, he suddenly has nowhere to hide. He might be Canadian, but the last time he skated he was ten, and no, he doesn't have hockey in his blood. With only a month until filming starts, he about to be exposed, but partnered with a player who's supposed to be giving him tips, he doesn't realize how many of his secrets will come to light. Falling in lust, one heated kiss at a time, is inevitable, but giving Cameron up at the end of the shoot could break his heart.

Cameron Chavkin is the face of the LA Storm. And the body, and the hair, and the smile. He's at the prime of his career, men and women want to be with him, and he's skating better than he ever has before. His house sits next to a famous rock star's mansion, his garage is filled with expensive cars, and he's even been asked to mentor a once-famous actor in a new hockey movie. Life is pretty sweet. Until the bad boy of hockey meets Finn, a man on the edge with more secrets than Cameron has endorsements. Knowing better than to get involved, Cameron is swept up despite himself, and when it's time to say goodbye to the Storm's most eligible bachelor is finding it hard to follow the script.

Script

LA Storm

1. Script
2. Second
3. Shield
4. Spiral

Off The Ice (Chesterford Coyotes, 1)

Off The Ice

A coming-of-age love story with high school, hockey rivalry, friendship, family, and coming out.

Soren's life changes in an instant when he and his younger brother are adopted by hockey royalty. Making sense of his new life is hard enough, but when he's enrolled in a private school it means facing a whole new set of problems. Navigating friendship, family, and hockey is one thing, but being attracted to the boy who vexes him is a whole new thing.

Felix has a reputation to protect. He's the kid who seems to have everything but looks can be deceiving. Spinning lies about his perfect life, he's created a fantasy world that even he has started to believe. Only, it's not long before everything crumbles, all of his pretty lies are revealed, and only his closest rival sees through his pain and stands by him.

Fighting is easy, friendship is hard, but love is everything.

Off The Ice

Chesterford Coyotes

1. Off The Ice
2. On Thin Ice
3. *Dance on Ice*

Also By RJ Scott

For a full list of ebooks and links please scan the code above or visit rjscott.co.uk/rjbooks

Meet RJ Scott

RJ discovered romance in books at a very young age and realized that if there wasn't romance on the page, she could create it in her head. With over one hundred and fifty books published, she is a full time author of gay romance.

She lives and works out of her home in the beautiful English countryside, spends her spare time reading, watching films, and enjoying time with her family.

The last time she had a week's break from writing she didn't like it one little bit and has yet to meet a box of chocolates she couldn't defeat.

www.rjscott.co.uk | rj@rjscott.co.uk

NEWSLETTER - rjscott.co.uk/rjnews

f facebook.com/author.rjscott

X x.com/Rjscott_author

instagram.com/rjscott_author

a amazon.com/author/rj-scott

BB bookbub.com/authors/rj-scott

g goodreads.com/rjscott

pinterest.com/rjscottauthor

Also By VL Locey

For a full list of ebooks and links please scan the code above or
visit vllocey.com/stories-from-vl-locey

Meet V.L. Locey

V.L. Locey loves worn jeans, yoga, belly laughs, walking, reading and writing lusty tales, Greek mythology, the New York Rangers, comic books, and coffee.

(Not necessarily in that order.)

She shares her life with her husband, her daughter, one dog, two cats, a flock of assorted domestic fowl, and two Jersey steers.

When not writing spicy romances, she enjoys spending her day with her menagerie in the rolling hills of Pennsylvania with a cup of fresh java in hand.

vllocey.com
vicki@vllocey.com

Newsletter - vllocey.com/newsletter

facebook.com/V.L.Locey
x.com/vllocey
instagram.com/vl_locey
bookbub.com/authors/v-l-locey
goodreads.com/vllocey
pinterest.com/vllocey